The Invisible Man

H.G. Wells

ALMA CLASSICS

ALMA CLASSICS
an imprint of

ALMA BOOKS LTD
3 Castle Yard
Richmond
Surrey TW10 6TF
United Kingdom
www.almaclassics.com

The Invisible Man first published in 1897
This edition first published by Alma Classics in 2017

Extra Material © Alma Books Ltd

Cover design: nathanburtondesign.com

Printed in Great Britain by CPI Group (UK) Ltd, Croydon CR0 4YY

ISBN: 978-1-84749-629-4

Contents

The Invisible Man   1
 Note on the Text   176
 Notes   176

Extra Material   181
 H.G. Wells's Life   183
 H.G. Wells's Works   192
 Select Bibliography   199

The Invisible Man

1

The Strange Man's Arrival

THE STRANGER CAME EARLY IN FEBRUARY, one wintry day, through a biting wind and a driving snow, the last snowfall of the year, over the down, walking from Bramblehurst railway station and carrying a little black portmanteau in his thickly gloved hand. He was wrapped up from head to foot, and the brim of his soft felt hat hid every inch of his face but the shiny tip of his nose; the snow had piled itself against his shoulders and chest, and added a white crest to the burden he carried. He staggered into the Coach and Horses more dead than alive, and flung his portmanteau down. "A fire," he cried, "in the name of human charity! A room and a fire!" He stamped and shook the snow from off himself in the bar, and followed Mrs Hall into her guest parlour to strike his bargain. And with that much introduction – that and a couple of sovereigns flung upon the table – he took up his quarters in the inn.

Mrs Hall lit the fire and left him there while she went to prepare him a meal with her own hands. A guest to stop at Iping in the wintertime was an unheard-of piece of luck, let alone a guest who was no "haggler", and she was resolved to show herself worthy of her good fortune.

As soon as the bacon was well under way, and Millie, her lymphatic aid, had been brisked up a bit by a few deftly chosen expressions of contempt, she carried the cloth, plates and glasses into the parlour and began to lay them with the utmost éclat. Although the fire was burning up briskly, she was surprised to see that her visitor still wore his hat and coat, standing with his back to her and staring out of the window at the falling snow in the yard.

His gloved hands were clasped behind him, and he seemed to be lost in thought. She noticed that the melted snow that still sprinkled his shoulders dripped upon her carpet.

"Can I take your hat and coat, sir," she said, "and give them a good dry in the kitchen?"

"No," he said, without turning.

She was not sure she had heard him, and was about to repeat her question.

He turned his head and looked at her over his shoulder. "I prefer to keep them on," he said with emphasis, and she noticed that he wore big blue spectacles with sidelights, and had a bushy side whisker over his coat collar that completely hid his cheeks and face.

"Very well, sir," she said. "*As* you like. In a bit the room will be warmer."

He made no answer, and had turned his face away from her again; and Mrs Hall, feeling that her conversational advances were ill timed, laid the rest of the table things in a quick staccato manner and whisked out of the room. When she returned he was still standing there like a man of stone, his back hunched, his collar turned up, his dripping hat brim turned down, hiding his face and ears completely. She put down the eggs and bacon with considerable emphasis, and called rather than said to him, "Your lunch is served, sir."

"Thank you," he said at the same time, and did not stir until she was closing the door. Then he swung round and approached the table.

As she went behind the bar to the kitchen, she heard a sound repeated at regular intervals. Chirk, chirk, chirk, it went, the sound of a spoon being rapidly whisked round a basin. "That girl!" she said. "There! I clean forgot it. It's her being so long!" And while she herself finished mixing the mustard, she gave Millie a few verbal stabs for her excessive slowness. She had cooked the ham and eggs, laid the table and done everything, while Millie (help indeed!) had only succeeded in delaying the mustard. And him a new guest and wanting to stay! Then she filled the mustard pot and, putting it with a certain stateliness upon a gold and black tea tray, carried it into the parlour.

She rapped and entered promptly. As she did so, her visitor moved quickly, so that she got but a glimpse of a white object disappearing behind the table. It would seem he was picking something from the floor. She rapped down the mustard pot on the table, and then she noticed the overcoat and hat had been taken off and put over a chair in front of the fire. A pair of wet boots threatened rust to her steel fender. She went to these things resolutely. "I suppose I may have them to dry now," she said in a voice that brooked no denial.

"Leave the hat," said her visitor in a muffled voice, and turning she saw he had raised his head and was sitting looking at her.

For a moment she stood gaping at him, too surprised to speak.

He held a white cloth – it was a serviette he had brought with him – over the lower part of his face, so that his mouth and jaws were completely hidden, and that was the reason of his muffled

5

voice. But it was not that which startled Mrs Hall. It was the fact that all his forehead above his blue glasses was covered by a white bandage, and that another covered his ears, leaving not a scrap of his face exposed excepting only his pink, peaked nose. It was bright pink, and shiny just as it had been at first. He wore a dark-brown velvet jacket with a high black linen-lined collar turned up about his neck. The thick black hair, escaping as it could below and between the cross bandages, projected in curious tails and horns, giving him the strangest appearance conceivable. This muffled and bandaged head was so unlike what she had anticipated that for a moment she was rigid.

He did not remove the serviette, but remained holding it, as she saw now, with a brown gloved hand, and regarding her with his inscrutable blue glasses. "Leave the hat," he said, speaking very distinctly through the white cloth.

Her nerves began to recover from the shock they had received. She placed the hat on the chair again by the fire. "I didn't know, sir," she began, "that..." and she stopped embarrassed.

"Thank you," he said drily, glancing from her to the door and then at her again.

"I'll have them nicely dried, sir, at once," she said, and carried his clothes out of the room. She glanced at his white-swathed head and blue goggles again as she was going out of the door, but his napkin was still in front of his face. She shivered a little as she closed the door behind her, and her face was eloquent of her surprise and perplexity. "I never," she whispered. "There!" She went quite softly to the kitchen, and was too preoccupied to ask Millie what she was messing about with *now*, when she got there.

The visitor sat and listened to her retreating feet. He glanced enquiringly at the window before he removed his serviette and resumed his meal. He took a mouthful, glanced suspiciously at the window, took another mouthful, then rose and, taking the serviette in his hand, walked across the room and pulled the blind down to the top of the white muslin that obscured the lower panes. This left the room in twilight. This done, he returned with an easier air to the table and his meal.

"The poor soul's had an accident or an op'ration or something," said Mrs Hall. "What a turn them bandages did give me, to be sure!"

She put on some more coal, unfolded the clothes horse and extended the traveller's coat upon this. "And they goggles! Why, he looked more like a divin' helmet than a human man!" She hung his muffler on a corner of the horse. "And holding that handkercher over his mouth all the time. Talkin' through it!... Perhaps his mouth was hurt too – maybe."

She turned round, as one who suddenly remembers. "Bless my soul alive!" she said, going off at a tangent. "Ain't you done them taters *yet*, Millie?"

When Mrs Hall went to clear away the stranger's lunch, her idea that his mouth must also have been cut or disfigured in the accident she supposed him to have suffered was confirmed, for he was smoking a pipe, and all the time that she was in the room he never loosened the silk muffler he had wrapped round the lower part of his face to put the mouthpiece to his lips. Yet it was not forgetfulness, for she saw he glanced at it as it smouldered out. He sat in the corner with his back to the window blind and spoke now, having eaten and drunk and being comfortably warmed through, with less aggressive brevity than before. The reflection of the fire lent a kind of red animation to his big spectacles they had lacked hitherto.

"I have some luggage," he said, "at Bramblehurst station," and he asked her how he could have it sent. He bowed his bandaged head quite politely in acknowledgement of her explanation. "Tomorrow!" he said. "There is no speedier delivery?" and seemed quite disappointed when she answered, "No." Was she quite sure? No man with a trap who would go over?

Mrs Hall, nothing loath, answered his questions and developed a conversation. "It's a steep road by the down, sir," she said in answer to the question about a trap; and then, snatching at an opening, said, "It was there a carriage was upsettled, a year ago and more. A gentleman killed, besides his coachman. Accidents, sir, happen in a moment, don't they?"

But the visitor was not to be drawn so easily. "They do," he said through his muffler, eyeing her quietly through his impenetrable glasses.

"But they take long enough to get well, sir, don't they?... There was my sister's son, Tom, jest cut his arm with a scythe, tumbled on it in the 'ayfield, and – bless me! – he was three months tied up, sir. You'd hardly believe it. It's regular given me a dread of a scythe, sir."

"I can quite understand that," said the visitor.

"He was afraid, one time, that he'd have to have an op'ration – he was that bad, sir."

The visitor laughed abruptly, a bark of a laugh that he seemed to bite and kill in his mouth. "*Was* he?" he said.

"He was, sir. And no laughing matter to them as had the doing for him, as I had – my sister being took up with her little ones so much. There was bandages to do, sir, and bandages to undo. So that if I may make so bold as to say it, sir—"

"Will you get me some matches?" said the visitor, quite abruptly. "My pipe is out."

Mrs Hall was pulled up suddenly. It was certainly rude of him, after telling him all she had done. She gasped at him for a moment, and remembered the two sovereigns. She went for the matches.

"Thanks," he said concisely, as she put them down, and turned his shoulder upon her and stared out of the window again. It was altogether too discouraging. Evidently he was sensitive on the topic of operations and bandages. She did not "make so bold as to say", after all. But his snubbing way had irritated her, and Millie had a hot time of it that afternoon.

The visitor remained in the parlour until four o'clock, without giving the ghost of an excuse for an intrusion. For the most part he was quite still during that time; it would seem he sat in the growing darkness smoking in the firelight, perhaps dozing.

Once or twice a curious listener might have heard him at the coals, and for the space of five minutes he was audible pacing the room. He seemed to be talking to himself. Then the armchair creaked as he sat down again.

2

Mr Teddy Henfrey's First Impressions

A T FOUR O'CLOCK, when it was fairly dark and Mrs Hall was screwing up her courage to go in and ask her visitor if he would take some tea, Teddy Henfrey, the clock-jobber,* came into the bar.

"My sakes! Mrs Hall," said he, "but this is terrible weather for thin boots!" The snow outside was falling faster.

Mrs Hall agreed, and then noticed he had his bag with him. "Now you're here, Mr Teddy," said she, "I'd be glad if you'd give th' old clock in the parlour a bit of a look. 'Tis going, and it strikes well and hearty, but the hour hand won't do nuthin' but point at six."

And leading the way, she went across to the parlour door and rapped and entered.

Her visitor, she saw as she opened the door, was seated in the armchair before the fire, dozing it would seem, with his bandaged head drooping on one side. The only light in the room was the red glow from the fire – which lit his eyes like adverse railway signals, but left his downcast face in darkness – and the scanty vestiges of the day that came in through the open door. Everything was ruddy, shadowy and indistinct to her, the more so since she had just been lighting the bar lamp, and her eyes were dazzled. But for a second it seemed to her that the man she looked at had an enormous mouth wide open – a vast and incredible mouth that swallowed the whole of the lower portion of his face. It was the sensation of a moment: the white-bound head, the monstrous goggle eyes and this huge yawn below it. Then he stirred, started up in his chair, put up his hand. She opened the door wide, so that the room was lighter, and she saw him more clearly, with the muffler held to his face just as she had seen him hold the serviette before. The shadows, she fancied, had tricked her.

"Would you mind, sir, this man a-coming to look at the clock, sir?" she said, recovering from her momentary shock.

"Look at the clock?" he said, staring round in a drowsy manner and speaking over his hand, and then, getting more fully awake. "Certainly."

Mrs Hall went away to get a lamp, and he rose and stretched himself. Then came the light, and Mr Teddy Henfrey, entering, was confronted by this bandaged person. He was, he says, "taken aback".

"Good afternoon," said the stranger, regarding him, as Mr Henfrey says with a vivid sense of the dark spectacles, "like a lobster".

"I hope," said Mr Henfrey, "that it's no intrusion."

"None whatever," said the stranger. "Though I understand," he said, turning to Mrs Hall, "that this room is really to be mine for my own private use."

"I thought, sir," said Mrs Hall, "you'd prefer the clock..." She was going to say "mended".

"Certainly," said the stranger, "certainly – but, as a rule, I like to be alone and undisturbed.

"But I'm really glad to have the clock seen to," he said, seeing a certain hesitation in Mr Henfrey's manner. "Very glad." Mr Henfrey had intended to apologize and withdraw, but this anticipation reassured him. The stranger stood round with his back to the fireplace and put his hands behind his back. "And presently," he said, "when the clock-mending is over, I think I should like to have some tea. But not till the clock-mending is over."

Mrs Hall was about to leave the room – she made no conversational advances this time, because she did not want to be snubbed in front of Mr Henfrey – when her visitor asked her if she had made any arrangements about his boxes at Bramblehurst. She told him she had mentioned the matter to the postman, and that the carrier could bring them over on the morrow. "You are certain that is the earliest?" he said.

She was certain, with a marked coldness.

"I should explain," he added, "what I was really too cold and fatigued to do before, that I am an experimental investigator."

"Indeed, sir," said Mrs Hall, much impressed.

"And my baggage contains apparatus and appliances."

"Very useful things indeed they are, sir," said Mrs Hall.

"And I'm naturally anxious to get on with my enquiries."

"Of course, sir."

"My reason for coming to Iping," he proceeded, with a certain deliberation of manner, "was – a desire for solitude. I do not wish to be disturbed in my work. In addition to my work, an accident…"

"I thought as much," said Mrs Hall to herself.

"…necessitates a certain retirement. My eyes – are sometimes so weak and painful that I have to shut myself up in the dark for hours together. Lock myself up. Sometimes – now and then. Not at present, certainly. At such times the slightest disturbance, the entry of a stranger into the room, is a source of excruciating annoyance to me – it is well these things should be understood."

"Certainly, sir," said Mrs Hall. "And if I might make so bold as to ask—"

"That, I think, is all," said the stranger, with that quietly irresistible air of finality he could assume at will. Mrs Hall reserved her question and sympathy for a better occasion.

After Mrs Hall had left the room, he remained standing in front of the fire, glaring, so Mr Henfrey puts it, at the clock-mending. Mr Henfrey not only took off the hands of the clock, and the face, but extracted the works, and he tried to work in as slow and quiet and unassuming a manner as possible. He worked with the lamp close to him, and the green shade threw a brilliant light upon his hands, and upon the frame and wheels, and left the rest of the room shadowy. When he looked up, coloured patches swam in his eyes. Being constitution-ally of a curious nature, he had removed the works – a quite unnecessary proceeding – with the idea of delaying his depar-ture and perhaps falling into conversation with the stranger. But the stranger stood there, perfectly silent and still. So still it got on Henfrey's nerves. He felt alone in the room and looked up, and there, grey and dim, was the bandaged head and huge blue lenses staring fixedly, with a mist of green spots drifting in front of them. It was so uncanny-looking to Henfrey that for a minute they remained staring blankly at one another. Then Henfrey looked down again. Very uncomfortable position! One would like to say something. Should he remark that the weather was very cold for the time of year?

He looked up as if to take aim with that introductory shot. "The weather" – he began.

"Why don't you finish and go?" said the rigid figure, evidently in a state of painfully suppressed rage. "All you've got to do is to fix the hour hand on its axle. You're simply humbugging—"

"Certainly, sir – one minute more, sir. I overlooked…" And Mr Henfrey finished and went.

But he went off feeling excessively annoyed. "Damn it!" said Mr Henfrey to himself, trudging down the village through the thawing snow. "A man must do a clock at times, sure-*ly*."

And again: "Can't a man look at you? Ugly!"

And yet again: "Seemingly not. If the police was wanting you, you couldn't be more wropped and bandaged."

At Gleeson's corner he saw Hall, who had recently married the stranger's hostess at the Coach and Horses, and who now drove the Iping conveyance, when occasional people required it, to Sidderbridge Junction, coming towards him on his return from that place. Hall had evidently been "stopping a bit" at Sidderbridge, to judge by his driving. "'Ow do, Teddy?" he said, passing.

"You got a rum un up home!" said Teddy.

Hall very sociably pulled up. "What's that?" he asked.

"Rum-looking customer stopping at the Coach and Horses," said Teddy. "My sakes!"

And he proceeded to give Hall a vivid description of his grotesque guest. "Looks a bit like a disguise, don't it? I'd like to see a man's face if I had him stopping in *my* place," said Henfrey. "But women are that trustful – where strangers are concerned. He's took your rooms and he ain't even given a name, Hall."

"You don't say so!" said Hall, who was a man of sluggish apprehension.

"Yes," said Teddy. "By the week. Whatever he is, you can't get rid of him under the week. And he's got a lot of luggage coming tomorrow, so he says. Let's hope it won't be stones in boxes, Hall."

He told Hall how his aunt at Hastings had been swindled by a stranger with empty portmanteaux. Altogether he left Hall vaguely suspicious. "Get up, old girl," said Hall. "I s'pose I must see 'bout this."

Teddy trudged on his way with his mind considerably relieved.

Instead of "seeing 'bout it", however, Hall on his return was severely rated by his wife on the length of time he had spent in Sidderbridge, and his mild enquiries were answered snappishly and in a manner not to the point. But the seed of suspicion Teddy had sown germinated in the mind of Mr Hall in spite of these discouragements. "You wim' don't know everything," said Mr Hall, resolved to ascertain more about the personality of his guest at the earliest possible opportunity. And after the stranger had gone to bed, which he did about half-past nine, Mr Hall went aggressively into the parlour and looked very hard at his wife's furniture, just to show that the stranger wasn't master there, and scrutinized closely and a little contemptuously a sheet of mathematical computations the stranger had left. When retiring for the night he instructed Mrs Hall to look very closely at the stranger's luggage when it came next day.

"You mind your own business, Hall," said Mrs Hall, "and I'll mind mine."

She was all the more inclined to snap at Hall, because the stranger was undoubtedly an unusually strange sort of stranger, and she was by no means assured about him in her own mind. In the middle of the night she woke up dreaming of huge white heads like turnips, that came trailing after her at the end of interminable necks, and with vast black eyes. But being a sensible woman, she subdued her terrors and turned over and went to sleep again.

3

The Thousand and One Bottles

S O IT WAS THAT ON THE NINTH DAY of February, at the beginning of the thaw, this singular person fell out of infinity into Iping Village. Next day his luggage arrived through the slush. And very remarkable luggage it was. There were a couple of trunks indeed, such as a rational man might need, but in addition there were a box of books – big, fat books, of which some were just in an incomprehensible handwriting – and a dozen or more crates, boxes and cases, containing objects packed in straw, as it seemed to Hall, tugging with a casual curiosity at the straw – glass bottles. The stranger, muffled in hat, coat, gloves and wrapper, came out impatiently to meet Fearenside's cart, while Hall was having a word or so of gossip preparatory to helping bring them in. Out he came, not noticing Fearenside's dog, who was sniffing in a dilettante spirit at Hall's legs. "Come along with those boxes," he said. "I've been waiting long enough."

And he came down the steps towards the tail of the cart as if to lay hands on the smaller crate.

No sooner had Fearenside's dog caught sight of him, however, than it began to bristle and growl savagely, and when he rushed down the steps it gave an undecided hop, and then sprang straight at his hand. "Whup!" cried Hall, jumping back, for he was no hero with dogs, and Fearenside howled, "Lie down!" and snatched his whip.

They saw the dog's teeth had slipped the hand, heard a kick, saw the dog execute a flanking jump and get home on the stranger's leg, and heard the rip of his trousering. Then the finer end of Fearenside's whip reached his property, and the dog, yelping with dismay, retreated under the wheels of the wagon. It was all the business of a half-minute. No one spoke, everyone shouted. The stranger glanced swiftly at his torn glove and at his leg, made as if he would stoop to the latter, then turned and rushed up the steps into the inn. They heard him go headlong across the passage and up the uncarpeted stairs to his bedroom.

"You brute, you!" said Fearenside, climbing off the wagon with his whip in his hand, while the dog watched him through the wheel. "Come here!" said Fearenside – "You'd better."

Hall had stood gaping. "He wuz bit," said Hall. "I'd better go and see to en," and he trotted after the stranger. He met Mrs Hall in the passage. "Carrier's darg," he said, "bit en."

He went straight upstairs and, the stranger's door being ajar, he pushed it open and was entering without any ceremony, being of a naturally sympathetic turn of mind.

The blind was down and the room dim. He caught a glimpse of a most singular thing, what seemed a handless arm waving towards him, and a face of three huge indeterminate spots on white, very like the face of a pale pansy. Then he was struck violently in the chest, hurled back, and the door slammed in his face and locked all so rapidly that he had no time to observe. A waving of indecipherable shapes, a blow and a concussion. There he stood on the dark little landing, wondering what it might be that he had seen.

After a couple of minutes he rejoined the little group that had formed outside the Coach and Horses. There was Fearenside telling about it all over again for the second time; there was Mrs Hall saying his dog didn't have no business to bite her guests; there was Huxter, the general dealer from over the road, interrogative; and Sandy Wadgers from the forge, judicial; besides women and children – all of them saying fatuities: "Wouldn't let en bite *me*, I knows"; "'Tasn't right *have* such dargs"; "Whad 'e bite'n for then?"; and so forth.

Mr Hall, staring at them from the steps and listening, found it incredible that he had seen anything very remarkable happen upstairs. Besides, his vocabulary was altogether too limited for his impressions.

"He don't want no help, he says," he said in answer to his wife's enquiry. "We'd better be a-takin' of his luggage in."

"He ought to have it cauterized at once," said Mr Huxter, "especially if it's at all inflamed."

"I'd shoot en, that's what I'd do," said a lady in the group.

Suddenly the dog began growling again.

"Come along," cried an angry voice in the doorway, and there stood the muffled stranger with his collar turned up, and his hat brim bent down. "The sooner you get those things in the better I'll be pleased." It is stated by an anonymous bystander that his trousers and gloves had been changed.

"Was you hurt, sir?" said Fearenside. "I'm rare sorry the darg—"

"Not a bit," said the stranger. "Never broke the skin. Hurry up with those things."

He then swore to himself, so Mr Hall asserts.

Directly the first crate was carried into the parlour, in accordance with his directions, the stranger flung himself upon it with extraordinary eagerness, and began to unpack it, scattering the straw with an utter disregard of Mrs Hall's carpet. And from it he began to produce bottles – little fat bottles containing powders, small and slender bottles containing coloured and white fluids, fluted blue bottles labelled *Poison*, bottles with round bodies and slender necks, large green glass bottles, large white glass bottles, bottles with glass stoppers and frosted labels, bottles with fine corks, bottles with bungs, bottles with wooden caps, wine bottles, salad-oil bottles – putting them in rows on the chiffonier, on the mantel, on the table under the window, round the floor, on the bookshelf – everywhere. The chemist's shop in Bramblehurst could not boast half so many. Quite a sight it was. Crate after crate yielded bottles, until all six were empty and the table high with straw; the only things that came out of these crates besides the bottles were a number of test tubes and a carefully packed balance.

And directly the crates were unpacked, the stranger went to the window and set to work, not troubling in the least about the litter of straw, the fire which had gone out, the box of books outside, nor for the trunks and other luggage that had gone upstairs.

When Mrs Hall took his dinner in to him, he was already so absorbed in his work, pouring little drops out of the bottles into test tubes, that he did not hear her until she had swept away the bulk of the straw and put the tray on the table, with some little emphasis perhaps, seeing the state that the floor was in. Then he half turned his head and immediately turned it away again. But she saw he had removed his glasses; they were beside him on the table, and it seemed to her that his eye sockets were extraordinarily hollow. He put on his spectacles again, and then turned and faced her. She was about to complain of the straw on the floor when he anticipated her.

THE INVISIBLE MAN

"I wish you wouldn't come in without knocking," he said in the tone of abnormal exasperation that seemed so characteristic of him.

"I knocked, but seemingly—"

"Perhaps you did. But in my investigations – my really very urgent and necessary investigations – the slightest disturbance, the jar of a door – I must ask you—"

"Certainly, sir. You can turn the lock if you're like that, you know – any time."

"A very good idea," said the stranger.

"This stror, sir, if I might make so bold as to remark—"

"Don't. If the straw makes trouble put it down in the bill." And he mumbled at her – words suspiciously like curses.

He was so odd, standing there, so aggressive and explosive, bottle in one hand and test tube in the other, that Mrs Hall was quite alarmed. But she was a resolute woman. "In which case, I should like to know, sir, what you consider—"

"A shilling. Put down a shilling. Surely a shilling's enough?"

"So be it," said Mrs Hall, taking up the tablecloth and beginning to spread it over the table. "If you're satisfied, of course…"

He turned and sat down, with his coat collar towards her.

All the afternoon he worked with the door locked and, as Mrs Hall testifies, for the most part in silence. But once there was a concussion and a sound of bottles ringing together as though the table had been hit, and the smash of a bottle flung violently down, and then a rapid pacing athwart the room. Fearing "something was the matter", she went to the door and listened, not caring to knock.

"I can't go on," he was raving. "I *can't* go on. Three hundred thousand, four hundred thousand! The huge multitude!

Cheated! All my life it may take me! Patience! Patience indeed! Fool and liar!"

There was a noise of hobnails on the bricks in the bar, and Mrs Hall very reluctantly had to leave the rest of his soliloquy. When she returned the room was silent again, save for the faint crepitation of his chair and the occasional clink of a bottle. It was all over. The stranger had resumed work.

When she took in his tea she saw broken glass in the corner of the room under the concave mirror, and a golden stain that had been carelessly wiped. She called attention to it.

"Put it down in the bill," snapped her visitor. "For God's sake don't worry me. If there's damage done, put it down in the bill," and he went on ticking a list in the exercise book before him.

"I'll tell you something," said Fearenside, mysteriously. It was late in the afternoon, and they were in the little beer shop of Iping Hanger.

"Well?" said Teddy Henfrey.

"This chap you're speaking of, what my dog bit. Well – he's black. Leastways, his legs are. I seed through the tear of his trousers and the tear of his glove. You'd have expected a sort of pinky to show, wouldn't you? Well – there wasn't none. Just blackness. I tell you, he's as black as my hat."

"My sakes!" said Henfrey. "It's a rummy case altogether. Why, his nose is as pink as paint!"

"That's true," said Fearenside. "I knows that. And I tell 'e what I'm thinking. That marn's a piebald, Teddy. Black here and white there – in patches. And he's ashamed of it. He's a kind of half-breed, and the colour's come off patchy instead of mixing. I've heard of such things before. And it's the common way with horses, as anyone can see."

4

Mr Cuss Interviews the Stranger

I HAVE TOLD THE CIRCUMSTANCES of the stranger's arrival in Iping with a certain fullness of detail, in order that the curious impression he created may be understood by the reader. But excepting two odd incidents, the circumstances of his stay until the extraordinary day of the Club Festival may be passed over very cursorily. There were a number of skirmishes with Mrs Hall on matters of domestic discipline, but in every case until late in April, when the first signs of penury began, he overrode her by the easy expedient of an extra payment. Hall did not like him, and whenever he dared he talked of the advisability of getting rid of him; but he showed his dislike chiefly by concealing it ostentatiously, and avoiding his visitor as much as possible. "Wait till the summer," said Mrs Hall, sagely, "when the artisks are beginning to come. Then we'll see. He may be a bit overbearing, but bills settled punctual is bills settled punctual, whatever you like to say."

The stranger did not go to church, and indeed made no difference between Sunday and the irreligious days, even in costume. He worked, as Mrs Hall thought, very fitfully. Some days he would come down early and be continuously busy. On others he would rise late, pace his room, fretting audibly for hours together, smoke, sleep in the armchair by the fire. Communication with the world beyond the village he had none. His temper continued very uncertain: for the most part his manner was that of a man suffering under almost unendurable provocation, and once or twice things were snapped, torn, crushed or broken in spasmodic gusts of violence. He seemed under a chronic irritation of the greatest intensity. His habit of talking to himself in a low voice grew steadily upon him, but though Mrs Hall listened conscientiously she could make neither head nor tail of what she heard.

He rarely went abroad by day, but at twilight he would go out muffled up enormously, whether the weather were cold or not, and he chose the loneliest paths and those most overshadowed by trees and banks. His goggling spectacles and ghastly bandaged face under the penthouse of his hat came with a disagreeable suddenness out of the darkness upon one or two home-going labourers; and Teddy Henfrey, tumbling out of the Scarlet Coat one night at half-past nine, was scared shamefully by the stranger's skull-like head (he was walking hat in hand) lit by the sudden light of the opened inn door. Such children as saw him at nightfall dreamt of bogies, and it seemed doubtful whether he disliked boys more than they disliked him, or the reverse – but there was certainly a vivid enough dislike on either side.

It was inevitable that a person of so remarkable an appearance and bearing should form a frequent topic in such a village as Iping. Opinion was greatly divided about his occupation. Mrs Hall was sensitive on the point. When questioned, she explained very carefully that he was an "experimental investigator", going gingerly over the syllables as one who dreads pitfalls. When asked what an experimental investigator was, she would say with a touch of superiority that most educated people knew that, and would then explain that he "discovered things". Her visitor had had an accident, she said, which temporarily discoloured his face and hands, and being of a sensitive disposition he was averse to any public notice of the fact.

Out of her hearing there was a view largely entertained that he was a criminal trying to escape from justice by wrapping himself up so as to conceal himself altogether from the eye of the police. This idea sprang from the brain of Mr Teddy Henfrey. No crime of any magnitude dating from the middle or end of February was known to have occurred. Elaborated in the imagination of Mr Gould, the probationary assistant in the National School,* this theory took the form that the stranger was an anarchist in disguise, preparing explosives, and here solved to undertake such detective operations as his time permitted. These consisted for the most part in looking very hard at the stranger whenever they met, or in asking people who had never seen the stranger leading questions about him. But he detected nothing.

Another school of opinion followed Mr Fearenside, and either accepted the piebald view or some modification of it; as, for instance, Silas Durgan, who was heard to assert that "if he choses to show enself at fairs he'd make his fortune in no time" and, being a bit of a theologian, compared the stranger to the man with the one talent.* Yet another view explained the entire matter by regarding the stranger as a harmless lunatic. That had the advantage of accounting for everything straight away.

Between these main groups there were waverers and compromisers. Sussex folk have few superstitions, and it was only after the events of early April that the thought of the supernatural was first whispered in the village. Even then it was only credited among the womenfolk.

But whatever they thought of him, people in Iping on the whole agreed in disliking him. His irritability, though it might have been comprehensible to an urban brain-worker, was an

amazing thing to these quiet Sussex villagers. The frantic gestic-
ulations they surprised now and then, the headlong pace after
nightfall that swept him upon them round quiet corners, the
inhuman bludgeoning of all the tentative advances of curiosity,
the taste for twilight that led to the closing of doors, the pulling down of blinds, the extinction of candles and lamps – who
could agree with such goings-on? They drew aside as he passed
down the village, and when he had gone by, young humorists
would up with coat collars and down with hat brims, and go
pacing nervously after him in imitation of his occult bearing.
There was a song popular at that time called the 'Bogey Man':
Miss Satchell sang it at the schoolroom concert (in aid of the
church lamps), and thereafter whenever one or two of the villagers were gathered together and the stranger appeared, a bar
or so of this tune, more or less sharp or flat, was whistled in the
midst of them. Also belated little children would call "Bogey
Man!" after him, and make off tremulously elated.

Cuss, the general practitioner, was devoured by curiosity.
The bandages excited his professional interest, the report of
the thousand and one bottles aroused his jealous regard. All
through April and May he coveted an opportunity of talking to
the stranger, and at last, towards Whitsuntide,* he could stand it
no longer, and hit upon the subscription list for a village nurse
as an excuse. He was surprised to find that Mr Hall did not
know his guest's name. "He give a name," said Mrs Hall – an
assertion which was quite unfounded, "but I didn't rightly hear
it." She thought it seemed so silly not to know the man's name.

Cuss rapped at the parlour door and entered. There was a
fairly audible imprecation from within. "Pardon my intrusion,"
said Cuss, and then the door closed and cut Mrs Hall off from
the rest of the conversation.

She could hear the murmur of voices for the next ten minutes, then a cry of surprise, a stirring of feet, a chair flung aside, a bark of laughter, quick steps to the door, and Cuss appeared, his face white, his eyes staring over his shoulder. He left the door open behind him and, without looking at her, strode across the hall and went down the steps, and she heard his feet hurrying along the road. He carried his hat in his hand. She stood behind the door, looking at the open door of the parlour. Then she heard the stranger laughing quietly, and then his footsteps came across the room. She could not see his face where she stood. The parlour door slammed, and the place was silent again.

Cuss went straight up the village to Bunting the vicar. "Am I mad?" Cuss began abruptly, as he entered the shabby little study. "Do I look like an insane person?"

"What's happened?" said the vicar, putting the ammonite on the loose sheets of his forthcoming sermon.

"That chap at the inn—"

"Well?"

"Give me something to drink," said Cuss, and he sat down.

When his nerves had been steadied by a glass of cheap sherry – the only drink the good vicar had available – he told him of the interview he had just had. "Went in," he gasped, "and began to demand a subscription for that nurse fund. He'd stuck his hands in his pockets as I came in, and he sat down lumpily in his chair. Sniffed. I told him I'd heard he took an interest in scientific things. He said yes. Sniffed again. Kept on sniffing all the time – evidently recently caught an infernal cold. No wonder, wrapped up like that! I developed the nurse idea, and all the while kept my eyes open. Bottles – chemicals – everywhere. Balance, test tubes in stands and a smell of – evening primrose. Would he subscribe? Said he'd consider it. Asked him, point-blank, was he researching. Said he was. A long research? Got quite cross. 'A damnable long research,' said he, blowing the cork out, so to speak. 'Oh,' said I. And out came the grievance. The man was just on the boil, and my question boiled him over. He had been given a prescription, most valuable prescription – what for he wouldn't say. Was it medical? 'Damn you! What are you fishing after?' I apologized. Dignified sniff and cough. He resumed. He'd read it. Five ingredients. Put it down, turned his head. Draught of air from window lifted the paper. Swish, rustle. He was working in a room with an open fireplace, he said. Saw a flicker, and there was the prescription burning and lifting chimney-ward. Rushed towards it just as it whisked up-chimney. So! Just at that point, to illustrate his story, out came his arm."

"Well?"

"No hand – just an empty sleeve. Lord! I thought, *that's* a deformity! Got a cork arm, I suppose, and has taken it off. Then, I thought, there's something odd in that. What the devil keeps that sleeve up and open, if there's nothing in it? There was nothing in it, I tell you. Nothing down it, right down to the joint. I could see right down it to the elbow, and there was a glimmer of light shining through a tear of the cloth. 'Good God!' I said. Then he stopped. Stared at me with those black goggles of his, and then at his sleeve."

"Well?"

"That's all. He never said a word; just glared, and put his sleeve back in his pocket quickly. 'I was saying,' said he, 'that there was the prescription burning, wasn't I?' Interrogative cough. 'How the devil,' said I, 'can you move an empty sleeve like that?' 'Empty sleeve?' 'Yes,' said I, 'an empty sleeve.'

"'It's an empty sleeve, is it? You saw it was an empty sleeve?' He stood up right away. I stood up too. He came towards me in three very slow steps and stood quite close. Sniffed venom-ously. I didn't flinch, though I'm hanged if that bandaged knob of his, and those blinkers, aren't enough to unnerve anyone, coming quietly up to you.

"'You said it was an empty sleeve?' he said. 'Certainly,' I said. At staring and saying nothing a barefaced man, unspectacled, starts scratch.* Then very quietly he pulled his sleeve out of his pocket again, and raised his arm towards me as though he would show it to me again. He did it very, very slowly. I looked at it. Seemed an age. 'Well?' said I, clearing my throat. 'There's nothing in it.' Had to say something. I was beginning to feel frightened. I could see right down it. He extended it straight towards me, slowly, slowly – just like that – until the cuff was six inches from my face. Queer thing to see an empty sleeve come at you like that! And then—"

"Well?"

"Something – exactly like a finger and thumb it felt – nipped my nose."

Bunting began to laugh.

"There wasn't anything there!" said Cuss, his voice running up into a shriek at the "there". "It's all very well for you to laugh, but I tell you I was so startled I hit his cuff hard, and turned round, and cut out of the room – I left him—"

Cuss stopped. There was no mistaking the sincerity of his panic. He turned round in a helpless way and took a second glass of the excellent vicar's very inferior sherry. "When I hit his cuff," said Cuss, "I tell you, it felt exactly like hitting an arm. And there wasn't an arm! There wasn't the ghost of an arm!"

Mr Bunting thought it over. He looked suspiciously at Cuss. "It's a most remarkable story," he said. He looked very wise and grave indeed. "It's really," said Mr Bunting with judicial emphasis, "a most remarkable story."

5

The Burglary at the Vicarage

THE FACTS OF THE BURGLARY at the vicarage come to us chiefly through the medium of the vicar and his wife. It occurred in the small hours of Whit Monday, the day devoted in Iping to the Club festivities. Mrs Bunting, it seems, woke up suddenly in the stillness that comes before the dawn, with the strong impression that the door of their bedroom had opened and closed. She did not arouse her husband at first, but sat up in bed listening. She then distinctly heard the pad, pad, pad of bare feet coming out of the adjoining dressing room and walking along the passage towards the staircase. As soon as she felt assured of this, she aroused the Rev. Mr Bunting as quietly as possible. He did not strike a light but, putting on his spectacles, her dressing gown and his bath slippers, he went out on the landing to listen. He heard quite distinctly a fumbling going on at his study desk downstairs, and then a violent sneeze.

At that he returned to his bedroom, armed himself with the most obvious weapon, the poker, and descended the staircase as noiselessly as possible. Mrs Bunting came out on the landing.

The hour was about four, and the ultimate darkness of the night was past. There was a faint shimmer of light in the hall, but the study doorway yawned impenetrably black. Everything was still except the faint creaking of the stairs under Mr Bunting's tread, and the slight movements in the study. Then something snapped, the drawer was opened and there was a rustle of papers. Then came an imprecation, and a match was struck and the study was flooded with yellow light. Mr Bunting was now in the hall, and through the crack of the door he could see the desk and the open drawer and a candle burning on the desk. But the robber he could not see. He stood there in the hall undecided what to do, and Mrs Bunting, her face white and intent, crept slowly downstairs after him. One thing kept up Mr Bunting's courage: the persuasion that this burglar was a resident in the village.

They heard the chink of money, and realized that the robber had found the housekeeping reserve of gold – two pounds ten in half-sovereigns altogether. At that sound Mr Bunting was nerved to abrupt action. Gripping the poker firmly, he rushed into the room, closely followed by Mrs Bunting. "Surrender!" cried Mr Bunting fiercely, and then stopped amazed. Apparently the room was perfectly empty.

Yet their conviction that they had, that very moment, heard somebody moving in the room had amounted to a certainty. For half a minute, perhaps, they stood gaping, then Mrs Bunting went across the room and looked behind the screen, while Mr Bunting, by a kindred impulse, peered under the desk. Then Mrs Bunting turned back the window curtains, and Mr Bunting looked up the chimney and probed it with the poker. Then Mrs Bunting scrutinized the waste-paper basket and Mr Bunting opened the lid of the coal scuttle. Then they came to a stop and stood with eyes interrogating each other.

"I could have sworn..." said Mr Bunting.

"The candle!" said Mr Bunting. "Who lit the candle?"

"The drawer!" said Mrs Bunting. "And the money's gone!"

She went hastily to the doorway.

CHAPTER 5

"Of all the extraordinary occurrences…"

There was a violent sneeze in the passage. They rushed out, and as they did so the kitchen door slammed. "Bring the candle," said Mr Bunting, and led the way. They both heard a sound of bolts being hastily shot back.

As he opened the kitchen door he saw through the scullery that the back door was just opening, and the faint light of early dawn displayed the dark masses of the garden beyond. He is certain that nothing went out of the door. It opened, stood open for a moment, and then closed with a slam. As it did so, the candle Mrs Bunting was carrying from the study flickered and flared. It was a minute or more before they entered the kitchen.

The place was empty. They refastened the back door, examined the kitchen, pantry and scullery thoroughly, and at last went down into the cellar. There was not a soul to be found in the house, search as they would.

Daylight found the vicar and his wife, a quaintly costumed little couple, still marvelling about on their own ground floor by the unnecessary light of a guttering candle.

6

The Furniture That Went Mad

NOW IT HAPPENED that in the early hours of Whit Monday, before Millie was hunted out for the day, Mr Hall and Mrs Hall both rose and went noiselessly down into the cellar. Their business there was of a private nature, and had something to do with the specific gravity of their beer. They had hardly entered the cellar when Mrs Hall found she had forgotten to bring down a bottle of sarsaparilla from their joint room. As she was the expert and principal operator in this affair, Hall very properly went upstairs for it.

On the landing he was surprised to see that the stranger's door was ajar. He went on into his own room and found the bottle as he had been directed.

But returning with the bottle, he noticed that the bolts of the front door had been shot back, that the door was in fact simply on the latch. And with a flash of inspiration he connected this with the stranger's room upstairs and the suggestions of Mr Teddy Henfrey. He distinctly remembered holding the candle while Mrs Hall shot these bolts overnight. At the sight he stopped, gaping, then, with the bottle still in his hand, went upstairs again. He rapped at the stranger's door. There was no answer. He rapped again, then pushed the door wide open and entered.

It was as he expected. The bed, the room also, was empty. And what was stranger, even to his heavy intelligence, on the bedroom chair and along the rail of the bed were scattered the garments, the only garments so far as he knew, and the bandages of their guest. His big slouch hat even was cocked jauntily over the bedpost.

As Hall stood there he heard his wife's voice coming out of the depth of the cellar, with that rapid telescoping of the syllables and interrogative cocking-up of the final words to a high note, by which the West Sussex villager is wont to indicate a brisk impatience. "Gearge! You gart what a wand?"

At that he turned and hurried down to her. "Janny," he said, over the rail of the cellar steps, "'tas the truth what Henfrey sez. 'E's not in uz room, 'e ent. And the front door's unbolted."

At first Mrs Hall did not understand, and as soon as she did she resolved to see the empty room for herself. Hall, still holding the bottle, went first. "If 'e ent there," he said, "his close are. And what's 'e doin' without his close, then? 'Tas a most curious basness."

As they came up the cellar steps, they both, it was afterwards ascertained, fancied they heard the front door open and shut, but seeing it closed and nothing there, neither said a word to the other about it at the time. Mrs Hall passed her husband in the passage and ran on first upstairs. Someone sneezed on the staircase. Hall, following six steps behind, thought that he heard her sneeze. She, going on first, was under the impression that Hall was sneezing. She flung open the door and stood regarding the room. "Of all the curious!" she said.

She heard a sniff close behind her head as it seemed, and, turning, was surprised to see Hall a dozen feet off on the topmost stair. But in another moment he was beside her. She

33

bent forward and put her hand on the pillow and then under the clothes.

"Cold," she said. "He's been up this hour or more."

As she did so, a most extraordinary thing happened – the bedclothes gathered themselves together, leapt up suddenly into a sort of peak and then jumped headlong over the bottom rail. It was exactly as if a hand had clutched them in the centre and flung them aside. Immediately after, the stranger's hat hopped off the bedpost, described a whirling flight in the air through the better part of a circle and then dashed straight at Mrs Hall's face. Then as swiftly came the sponge from the washstand; and then the chair, flinging the stranger's coat and trousers carelessly aside, and laughing drily in a voice singularly like the stranger's, turned itself up with its four legs at Mrs Hall, seemed to take aim at her for a moment and charged at her. She screamed and turned, and then the chair legs came gently but firmly against her back and impelled her and Hall out of the room. The door slammed violently and was locked. The chair and bed seemed to be executing a dance of triumph for a moment, and then abruptly everything was still.

Mrs Hall was left almost in a fainting condition in Mr Hall's arms on the landing. It was with the greatest difficulty that Mr Hall and Millie, who had been roused by her scream of alarm, succeeded in getting her downstairs and applying the restoratives customary in these cases.

"'Tas sperrits," said Mrs Hall. "I know 'tas sperrits. I've read in papers of en. Tables and chairs leaping and dancing!"

"Take a drop more, Janny," said Hall. "'Twill steady ye."

"Lock him out," said Mrs Hall. "Don't let him come in again. I half-guessed – I might ha' known. With them goggling eyes and bandaged head, and never going to church of a Sunday.

CHAPTER 6

And all they bottles – more'n it's right for anyone to have. He's put the sperrits into the furniture – my good old furniture! 'Twas in that very chair my poor dear mother used to sit when I was a little girl. To think it should rise up against me now!"

"Just a drop more, Janny," said Hall. "Your nerves is all upset."

They sent Millie across the street through the golden five-o'clock sunshine to rouse up Mr Sandy Wadgers, the blacksmith. Mr Hall's compliments and the furniture upstairs was behaving most extraordinary. Would Mr Wadgers come round? He was a knowing man, was Mr Wadgers, and very resourceful. He took quite a grave view of the case. "Arm darmed ef thet ent witchcraft," was the view of Mr Sandy Wadgers. "You warnt horseshoes for such gentry as he."

He came round greatly concerned. They wanted him to lead the way upstairs to the room, but he didn't seem to be in any hurry. He preferred to talk in the passage. Over the way Huxter's apprentice came out and began taking down the shutters of the tobacco window. He was called over to join the discussion. Mr Huxter naturally followed in the course of a few minutes. The Anglo-Saxon genius for parliamentary government asserted itself: there was a great deal of talk and no decisive action. "Let's have the facts first," insisted Mr Sandy Wadgers. "Let's be sure we'd be acting perfectly right in bustin' that there door open. A door onbust is always open to bustin', but ye can't onbust a door once you've busted en."

And suddenly and most wonderfully the door of the room upstairs opened of its own accord, and as they looked up in amazement they saw descending the stairs the muffled figure of the stranger staring more blackly and blankly than ever with those unreasonably large blue glass eyes of his. He came

35

down stiffly and slowly, staring all the time; he walked across the passage staring, then stopped.

"Look there!" he said, and their eyes followed the direction of his gloved finger and saw a bottle of sarsaparilla hard by the cellar door. Then he entered the parlour, and suddenly, swiftly, viciously, slammed the door in their faces.

Not a word was spoken until the last echoes of the slam had died away. They stared at one another. "Well, if that don't lick everything!" said Mr Wadgers, and left the alternative unsaid.

"I'd go in and ask'n 'bout it," said Wadgers, to Mr Hall. "I'd d'mand an explanation."

It took some time to bring the landlady's husband up to that pitch. At last he rapped, opened the door, and got as far as, "Excuse me—"

"Go to the devil!" said the stranger in a tremendous voice, and "Shut that door after you." So that brief interview terminated.

7

The Unveiling of the Stranger

T HE STRANGER WENT into the little parlour of the Coach and Horses about half-past five in the morning, and there he remained until near midday, the blinds down, the door shut and none, after Hall's repulse, venturing near him.

All that time he must have fasted. Thrice he rang his bell, the third time furiously and continuously, but no one answered him. "Him and his 'go to the devil' indeed!" said Mrs Hall. Presently came an imperfect rumour of the burglary at the vicarage, and two and two were put together. Hall, assisted by Wadgers, went off to find Mr Shuckleforth, the magistrate, and take his advice. No one ventured upstairs. How the stranger occupied himself is unknown. Now and then he would stride violently up and down, and twice came an outburst of curses, a tearing of paper and a violent smashing of bottles.

The little group of scared but curious people increased. Mrs Huxter came over; some gay young fellows resplendent in black ready-made jackets and piqué paper ties, for it was Whit Monday, joined the group with confused inter-rogations. Young Archie Harker distinguished himself by going up the yard and trying to peep under the window blinds. He could see nothing, but gave reason for suppos-ing that he did, and others of the Iping youth presently joined him.

It was the finest of all possible Whit Mondays, and down the village street stood a row of nearly a dozen booths and a shooting gallery, and on the grass by the forge were three yellow-and-chocolate wagons and some picturesque strangers of both sexes putting up a coconut shy. The gentlemen wore blue jerseys, the ladies white aprons and quite fashionable hats with heavy plumes. Wodger of the Purple Fawn and Mr Jaggers the cobbler, who also sold second-hand ordinary bicycles,* were stretching a string of Union Jacks and royal ensigns (which had originally celebrated the Jubilee*) across the road…

And inside, in the artificial darkness of the parlour, into which only one thin jet of sunlight penetrated, the stranger, hungry we must suppose, and fearful, hidden in his uncomfortable hot wrappings, pored through his dark glasses upon his paper or chinked his dirty little bottles, and occasionally swore savagely at the boys, audible if invisible, outside the windows. In the corner by the fireplace lay the fragments of half a dozen smashed bottles, and a pungent tang of chlorine tainted the air. So much we know from what was heard at the time and from what was subsequently seen in the room.

About noon he suddenly opened his parlour door and stood glaring fixedly at the three or four people in the bar. "Mrs Hall," he said. Somebody went sheepishly and called for Mrs Hall.

Mrs Hall appeared after an interval, a little short of breath, but all the fiercer for that. Hall was still out. She had deliberated over this scene, and she came holding a little tray with an unsettled bill upon it. "Is it your bill you're wanting, sir?" she said.

"Why wasn't my breakfast laid? Why haven't you prepared my meals and answered my bell? Do you think I live without eating?"

"Why isn't my bill paid?" said Mrs Hall. "That's what I want to know."

"I told you three days ago I was awaiting a remittance—"

"I told you two days ago I wasn't going to await no remittances. You can't grumble if your breakfast waits a bit, if my bill's been waiting these five days, can you?"

The stranger swore briefly but vividly.

"Nar, nar!" from the bar.

"And I'd thank you kindly, sir, if you'd keep your swearing to yourself, sir," said Mrs Hall.

The stranger stood looking more like an angry diving helmet than ever. It was universally felt in the bar that Mrs Hall had the better of him. His next words showed as much.

"Look here, my good woman—" he began.

"Don't good woman *me*," said Mrs Hall.

"I've told you my remittance hasn't come—"

"Remittance indeed!" said Mrs Hall.

"Still, I daresay in my pocket—"

"You told me two days ago that you hadn't anything but a sovereign's worth of silver upon you—"

"Well, I've found some more—"

"'Ul-*lo*!" from the bar.

"I wonder where you found it!" said Mrs Hall.

That seemed to annoy the stranger very much. He stamped his foot. "What do you mean?" he said.

"That I wonder where you found it," said Mrs Hall. "And before I take any bills or get any breakfasts, or do any such things whatsoever, you got to tell me one or two things I don't understand, and what nobody don't understand, and what everybody is very anxious to understand. I want know what you been doing t' my chair upstairs, and I want know how 'tis your room was empty, and how you got in again. Them as stops in this house comes in by the doors – that's the rule of the house, and that you *didn't* do, and what I want know is how you *did* come in. And I want know—"

Suddenly the stranger raised his gloved hands clenched, stamped his foot, and said, "Stop!" with such extraordinary violence that he silenced her instantly.

"You don't understand," he said, "who I am or what I am. I'll show you. By Heaven! I'll show you." Then he put his open palm over his face and withdrew it. The centre of his face became a black cavity. "Here," he said. He stepped forward and handed Mrs Hall something which she, staring at his metamorphosed face, accepted automatically. Then, when she saw what it was, she screamed loudly, dropped it, and staggered back. The nose – it was the stranger's nose! pink and shining – rolled on the floor.

Then he removed his spectacles, and everyone in the bar gasped. He took off his hat, and with a violent gesture tore at his whiskers and bandages. For a moment they resisted him. A flash of horrible anticipation passed through the bar. "Oh, my Gard!" said someone. Then off they came.

It was worse than anything. Mrs Hall, standing open-mouthed and horror-struck, shrieked at what she saw, and made for the door of the house. Everyone began to move. They were prepared for scars, disfigurements, tangible horrors, but *nothing*! The bandages and false hair flew across the passage into the bar, making a hobbledehoy jump to avoid them. Everyone tumbled on everyone else down the steps. For the man who stood there shouting some incoherent explanation was a solid gesticulating figure up to the coat collar of him, and then – nothingness, no visible thing at all!

People down the village heard shouts and shrieks, and looking up the street saw the Coach and Horses violently firing out its humanity. They saw Mrs Hall fall down and Mr Teddy Henfrey jump to avoid tumbling over her, and then they heard the frightful screams of Millie, who, emerging suddenly from the kitchen at the noise of the tumult, had come upon the headless stranger from behind.

Forthwith everyone all down the street – the sweetstuff seller, coconut-shy proprietor and his assistant, the swing man, little boys and girls, rustic dandies, smart wenches, smocked elders and aproned gypsies – began running towards the inn; and in a miraculously short space of time a crowd of perhaps forty people, and rapidly increasing, swayed and hooted and enquired and exclaimed and suggested, in front of Mrs Hall's establishment. Everyone seemed eager to talk at once, and the result was Babel.* A small group supported Mrs Hall, who was picked up in a state of collapse. There was a confusion, and the incredible evidence of a vociferous eyewitness. "O' Bogey!" "What's he been doin', then?" "Ain't hurt the girl, 'as 'e?" "Run at en with a knife, I believe." "No 'ed, I tell ye. I don't mean no manner of speaking, I mean *marn 'ithouta 'ed*!" "Narnsense! 'Tas some conjuring trick." "Fetched off 'is wrappin's, 'e did…"

In its struggles to see in through the open door, the crowd formed itself into a straggling wedge, with the more adventurous apex nearest the inn. "He stood for a moment, I heerd the gal scream, and he turned. I saw her skirts whisk, and he went after her. Didn't take ten seconds. Back he comes with a knife in uz hand and a loaf; stood just as if he was staring. Not a moment ago. Went in that there door. I tell 'e, 'e ain't gart no 'ed 't all. You just missed en…"

There was a disturbance behind, and the speaker stopped to step aside for a little procession that was marching very resolutely towards the house – first Mr Hall, very red and determined, then Mr Bobby Jaffers, the village constable, and then the wary Mr Wadgers. They had come now armed with a warrant.

People shouted conflicting information of the recent circumstances. "'Ed or no 'ed," said Jaffers, "I got to 'rest en, and 'rest en I *will*."

Mr Hall marched up the steps, marched straight to the door of the parlour and found it open. "Constable," he said, "do your duty."

Jaffers marched in, Hall next, Wadgers last. They saw in the dim light the headless figure facing them, with a gnawed crust of bread in one gloved hand and a chunk of cheese in the other.

"That's him!" said Hall.

"What the devil's this?" came in a tone of angry expostulation from above the collar of the figure.

"You're a damned rum customer, mister," said Mr Jaffers. "But 'ed or no 'ed, the warrant says 'body', and duty's duty—"

"Keep off!" said the figure, starting back.

Abruptly he whipped down the bread and cheese, and Mr Hall just grasped the knife on the table in time to save it. Off came the stranger's left glove and was slapped in Jaffers's face. In another moment Jaffers, cutting short some statement concerning a warrant, had gripped him by the handless wrist and caught his invisible throat. He got a sounding kick on the shin that made him shout, but he kept his grip. Hall sent the knife sliding along the table to Wadgers, who acted as goalkeeper for the offensive, so to speak, and then stepped forward as Jaffers and the stranger swayed and staggered towards him, clutching and hitting in. A chair stood in the way, and went aside with a crash as they came down together.

"Get the feet," said Jaffers between his teeth.

Mr Hall, endeavouring to act on instructions, received a sounding kick in the ribs that disposed of him for a moment, and Mr Wadgers, seeing the decapitated stranger had rolled over and got the upper side of Jaffers, retreated towards the door, knife in hand, and so collided with Mr Huxter and the Siddermorton carter coming to the rescue of law and order. At the same moment down came three or four bottles from the chiffonier and shot a web of pungency into the air of the room.

"I'll surrender," cried the stranger, though he had Jaffers down, and in another moment he stood up panting, a strange figure, headless and handless – for he had pulled off his right glove now as well as his left. "It's no good," he said, as if sobbing for breath.

It was the strangest thing in the world to hear that voice coming as if out of empty space, but the Sussex peasants are perhaps the most matter-of-fact people under the sun. Jaffers got up also and produced a pair of handcuffs. Then he started.

"I say!" said Jaffers, brought up short by a dim realization of the incongruity of the whole business. "Darm it! Can't use 'em as I can see."

The stranger ran his arm down his waistcoat, and as if by a miracle the buttons to which his empty sleeve pointed became undone. Then he said something about his shin and stooped down. He seemed to be fumbling with his shoes and socks.

"Why!" said Huxter, suddenly. "That's not a man at all. It's just empty clothes. Look! You can see down his collar and the linings of his clothes. I could put my arm…"

He extended his hand: it seemed to meet something in mid-air, and he drew it back with a sharp exclamation. "I wish you'd keep your fingers out of my eye," said the aerial voice, in a tone of savage expostulation. "The fact is, I'm all here: head, hands, legs and all the rest of it, but it happens I'm invisible. It's a confounded nuisance, but I am. That's no reason why I should be poked to pieces by every stupid bumpkin in Iping, is it?"

The suit of clothes, now all unbuttoned and hanging loosely upon its unseen supports, stood up, arms akimbo.

Several other of the menfolk had now entered the room, so that it was closely crowded. "Invisible, eh?" said Huxter, ignoring the stranger's abuse. "Whoever heard the likes of that?"

"It's strange, perhaps, but it's not a crime. Why am I assaulted by a policeman in this fashion?"

"Ah! That's a different matter," said Jaffers. "No doubt you are a bit difficult to see in this light, but I got a warrant and it's all correct. What I'm after ain't no invisibility – it's burglary. There's a house been broken into and money took."

"Well?"

"And circumstances certainly point—"

"Stuff and nonsense!" said the Invisible Man.

"I hope so, sir – but I've got my instructions."

"Well," said the stranger, "I'll come. I'll *come*. But no handcuffs."

"It's the regular thing," said Jaffers.

"No handcuffs," stipulated the stranger.

"Pardon me," said Jaffers.

Abruptly the figure sat down, and before anyone could realize what was being done, the slippers, socks and trousers had been kicked off under the table. Then he sprang up again and flung off his coat.

"Here, stop that," said Jaffers, suddenly realizing what was happening. He gripped the waistcoat; it struggled, and the shirt slipped out of it and left it limp and empty in his hand. "Hold him!" said Jaffers loudly. "Once he gets they things off!..."

"Hold him!" cried everyone, and there was a rush at the fluttering white shirt, which was now all that was visible of the stranger.

The shirtsleeve planted a shrewd blow in Hall's face that stopped his open-armed advance and sent him backwards into old Toothsome the sexton, and in another moment the garment was lifted up and became convulsed and vacantly flapping about the arms, even as a shirt that is being thrust off over a man's head. Jaffers clutched at it, and only helped to pull it off; he was struck in the mouth out of the air, and incontinently drew his truncheon and smote Teddy Henfrey savagely upon the crown of his head.

"Look out!" said everybody, fencing at random and hitting at nothing. "Hold him! Shut the door! Don't let him loose! I got something! Here he is!" A perfect Babel of noises they made. Everybody, it seemed, was being hit all at once, and Sandy Wadgers, knowing as ever and his wits sharpened by a frightful blow on the nose, reopened the door and led the rout. The others, following incontinently, were jammed for a moment in the corner by the doorway. The hitting continued. Phipps, the Unitarian,* had a front tooth broken, and Henfrey was injured in the cartilage of his ear. Jaffers was struck under the jaw and, turning, caught at something that intervened between him and Huxter in the mêlée, and prevented their coming together. He felt a muscular chest, and in another moment the whole mass of struggling, excited men shot out into the crowded hall.

"I got him!" shouted Jaffers, choking and reeling through them all and wrestling with purple face and swelling veins against his unseen enemy.

Men staggered right and left as the extraordinary conflict swayed swiftly towards the house door and went spinning down the half-dozen steps of the inn. Jaffers cried in a strangled voice – holding tight, nevertheless, and making play with his knee – spun round and fell heavily undermost with his head on the gravel. Only then did his fingers relax.

There were excited cries of "Hold him!" "Invisible!" and so forth, and a young fellow, a stranger in the place whose name did not come to light, rushed in at once, caught something, missed his hold and fell over the constable's prostrate body. Halfway across the road a woman screamed as something pushed by her; a dog, kicked apparently, yelped and ran howling into Huxter's yard, and with that the transit of the Invisible Man was accomplished. For a space people stood amazed and gesticulating, and then came panic and scattered them abroad through the village as a gust scatters dead leaves.

But Jaffers lay quite still, face upward and knees bent.

8

In Transit

T HE EIGHTH CHAPTER is exceedingly brief and relates that Gibbins, the amateur naturalist of the district, while lying out on the spacious open downs without a soul within a couple of miles of him, as he thought, and almost dozing, heard close to him the sound as of a man coughing, sneezing and then swearing savagely to himself; and, looking, beheld nothing. Yet the voice was indisputable. It continued to swear with that breadth and variety that distinguishes the swearing of a cultivated man. It grew to a climax, diminished again and died away in the distance, going as it seemed to him in the direction of Adderdean. It lifted to a spasmodic sneeze and ended. Gibbins had heard nothing of the morning's occurrences, but the phenomenon was so striking and disturbing that his philosophical tranquillity vanished; he got up hastily, and hurried down the steepness of the hill towards the village, as fast as he could go.

9

Mr Thomas Marvel

Y OU MUST PICTURE Mr Thomas Marvel as a person of copious, flexible visage, a nose of cylindrical protrusion, a liquorish, ample, fluctuating mouth and a beard of bristling eccentricity. His figure inclined to embonpoint; his short limbs accentuated this inclination. He wore a furry silk hat, and the frequent substitution of twine and shoelaces for buttons, apparent at critical points of his costume, marked a man essentially bachelor.

Mr Thomas Marvel was sitting with his feet in a ditch by the roadside over the down towards Adderdean, about a mile and a half out of Iping. His feet, save for socks of irregular openwork, were bare, his big toes were broad, and pricked like the ears of a watchful dog. In a leisurely manner – he did everything in a leisurely manner – he was contemplating trying on a pair of boots. They were the soundest boots he had come across for a long time, but too large for him; whereas the ones he had were, in dry weather, a very comfortable fit, but too thin-soled for damp. Mr Thomas Marvel hated roomy boots, but then he hated damp. He had never properly thought out which he hated most, and it was a pleasant day, and there was nothing better to do. So he put the four boots in a graceful group on the turf and looked at them. And seeing them there among the grass and springing agrimony, it suddenly occurred to him that both pairs were exceedingly ugly to see. He was not at all startled by a voice behind him.

"They're boots, anyhow," said the Voice.

"They are – charity boots," said Mr Thomas Marvel, with his head on one side regarding them distastefully, "and which is the ugliest pair in the whole blessed universe, I'm darned if I know!"

"H'm," said the Voice.

"I've worn worse – in fact, I've worn none. But none so owdacious ugly – if you'll allow the expression. I've been cadging boots – in particular – for days. Because I was sick of *them*. They're sound enough, of course. But a gentleman on tramp sees such a thundering lot of his boots. And if you'll believe me, I've raised nothing in the whole blessed county, try as I would, but THEM. Look at 'em! And a good county for boots, too, in a general way. But it's just my promiscuous luck. I've got my boots in this county ten years or more. And then they treat you like this."

"It's a beast of a county," said the Voice. "And pigs for people."

"Ain't it?" said Mr Thomas Marvel. "Lord! But them boots! It beats it."

He turned his head over his shoulder to the right, to look at the boots of his interlocutor with a view to comparisons, and – lo! – where the boots of his interlocutor should have been were neither legs nor boots. He turned his head over his shoulder to the left, and there also were neither legs nor boots. He was irradiated by the dawn of a great amazement. "Where *are* yer?" said Mr Thomas Marvel over his shoulder and coming round on all fours. He saw a stretch of empty down with the wind swaying the remote green-pointed furze bushes.

"Am I drunk?" said Mr Marvel. "Have I had visions? Was I talking to myself? What the—"

"Don't be alarmed," said a Voice.

"None of your ventriloquizing *me*," said Mr Thomas Marvel, rising sharply to his feet. "Where *are* yer? Alarmed, indeed!"

"Don't be alarmed," repeated the Voice.

"*You'll* be alarmed in a minute, you silly fool," said Mr Thomas Marvel. "Where *are* yer? Lemme get my mark on yer…

"Are you *buried?*" said Mr Thomas Marvel, after an interval.

There was no answer. Mr Thomas Marvel stood bootless and amazed, his jacket nearly thrown off.

"Peewit," said a peewit,* very remote.

"Peewit, indeed!" said Mr Thomas Marvel. "This ain't no time for foolery." The down was desolate, east and west, north and south; the road, with its shallow ditches and white bordering stakes, ran smooth and empty north and south and, save for that peewit, the blue sky was empty too. "So help me," said Mr Thomas Marvel, shuffling his coat onto his shoulders again. "It's the drink! I might ha' known."

"It's not the drink," said the Voice. "You keep your nerves steady."

"Ow!" said Mr Marvel, and his face grew white amidst its patches. "It's the drink," his lips repeated noiselessly. He remained staring about him, rotating slowly backwards. "I could have *swore* I heard a voice," he whispered.

"Of course you did."

"It's there again," said Mr Marvel, closing his eyes and clasping his hand on his brow with a tragic gesture. He was suddenly taken by the collar and shaken violently, and left more dazed than ever. "Don't be a fool," said the Voice.

"I'm – off – my – blooming – chump," said Mr Marvel. "It's no good. It's fretting about them blarsted boots. I'm off my blessed blooming chump. Or it's spirits."

"Neither one thing nor the other," said the Voice. "Listen!"

"Chump," said Mr Marvel.

"One minute," said the Voice penetratingly – tremulous, with self-control.

"Well?" said Mr Thomas Marvel, with a strange feeling of having been dug in the chest by a finger.

"You think I'm just imagination? Just imagination?"

"What else *can* you be?" said Mr Thomas Marvel, rubbing the back of his neck.

"Very well," said the Voice, in a tone of relief. "Then I'm going to throw flints at you till you think differently."

"But where *are* yer?"

The Voice made no answer. Whizz came a flint, apparently out of the air, and missed Mr Marvel's shoulder by a hair's breadth. Mr Marvel, turning, saw a flint jerk up into the air, trace a complicated path, hang for a moment and then fall at his feet with almost invisible rapidity. He was too amazed to dodge. Whizz it came, and ricocheted from a bare toe into the ditch. Mr Marvel jumped a foot and howled aloud. Then he started to run, tripped over an unseen obstacle and came head over heels into a sitting position.

"*Now*," said the Voice, as a third stone curved upwards and hung in the air above the tramp. "Am I imagination?"

Mr Marvel by way of reply struggled to his feet, and was immediately rolled over again. He lay quiet for a moment. "If you struggle any more," said the Voice, "I shall throw the flint at your head."

"It's a fair do," said Mr Thomas Marvel, sitting up, taking his wounded toe in hand and fixing his eye on the third missile. "I don't understand it. Stones flinging themselves. Stones talking. Put yourself down. Rot away. I'm done."

The third flint fell.

"It's very simple," said the Voice. "I'm an invisible man."

"Tell us something I don't know," said Mr Thomas Marvel, gasping with pain. "Where you've hid – how you do it – I *don't* know. I'm beat."

"That's all," said the Voice. "I'm invisible. That's what I want you to understand."

"Anyone could see that. There is no need for you to be so confounded impatient, mister. *Now* then. Give us a notion. How are you hid?"

"I'm invisible. That's the great point. And what I want you to understand is this—"

"But whereabouts?" interrupted Mr Marvel.

"Here! Six yards in front of you."

"Oh, *come*! I ain't blind. You'll be telling me next you're just thin air. I'm not one of your ignorant tramps—"

"Yes, I am – thin air. You're looking through me."

"What! Ain't there any stuff to you? *Vox et* – what is it? – jabber.* Is it that?"

"I am just a human being – solid, needing food and drink, needing covering too – but I'm invisible. You see? Invisible. Simple idea. Invisible."

"What, real like?"

"Yes, real."

"Let's have a hand of you," said Marvel, "if you *are* real. It won't be so darn out-of-the-way like, then – *Lord*!" he said. "How you made me jump! Gripping me like that!"

He felt the hand that had closed round his wrist with his disengaged fingers, and his touch went timorously up the arm, patted a muscular chest and explored a bearded face. Marvel's face was astonishment.

"I'm dashed!" he said. "If this don't beat cockfighting! Most remarkable! And there I can see a rabbit clean through you, 'arf a mile away! Not a bit of you visible – except…"

He scrutinized the apparently empty space keenly. "You 'aven't been eatin' bread and cheese?" he asked, holding the invisible arm.

"You're quite right, and it's not quite assimilated into the system."

"Ah!" said Mr Marvel. "Sort of ghostly, though."

"Of course, all this isn't half so wonderful as you think."

"It's quite wonderful enough for *my* modest wants," said Mr Thomas Marvel. "Howjer manage it! How the dooce is it done?"

"It's too long a story. And besides—"

"I tell you, the whole business fair beats me," said Mr Marvel.

"What I want to say at present is this: I need help. I have come to that… I came upon you suddenly. I was wandering, mad with rage, naked, impotent. I could have murdered. And I saw you—"

"*Lord!*" said Mr Marvel.

"I came up behind you – hesitated – went on…"

Mr Marvel's expression was eloquent.

"…then stopped. 'Here,' I said, 'is an outcast like myself. This is the man for me.' So I turned back and came to you – you. And—"

"*Lord!*" said Mr Marvel. "But I'm all in a dizzy. May I ask – how is it? And what you may be requiring in the way of help? Invisible!"

"I want you to help me get clothes – and shelter – and then, with other things. I've left them long enough. If you won't – well! But you *will – must*."

"Look here," said Mr Marvel. "I'm too flabbergasted. Don't knock me about any more. And leave me go. I must get steady a bit. And you've pretty near broken my toe. It's all so unreasonable. Empty downs, empty sky. Nothing visible for miles except the bosom of Nature. And then comes a voice. A voice out of heaven! And stones! And a fist – Lord!"

"Pull yourself together," said the Voice, "for you have to do the job I've chosen for you."

Mr Marvel blew out his cheeks, and his eyes were round.

"I've chosen you," said the Voice. "You are the only man except some of those fools down there, who knows there is such a thing as an invisible man. You have to be my helper. Help me – and I will do great things for you. An invisible man is a man of power." He stopped for a moment to sneeze violently.

"But if you betray me," he said, "if you fail to do as I direct you…"

He paused and tapped Mr Marvel's shoulder smartly. Mr Marvel gave a yelp of terror at the touch. "I don't want to betray you," said Mr Marvel, edging away from the direction of the fingers. "Don't you go a-thinking that, whatever you do. All I want to do is to help you – just tell me what I got to do. (Lord!) Whatever you want done, that I'm most willing to do."

10

Mr Marvel's Visit to Iping

AFTER THE FIRST GUSTY PANIC had spent itself, Iping became argumentative. Scepticism suddenly reared its head – rather nervous scepticism, not at all assured of its back, but scepticism nevertheless. It is so much easier not to believe in an invisible man, and those who had actually seen him dissolve into air, or felt the strength of his arm, could be counted on the fingers of two hands. And of these witnesses Mr Wadgers was presently missing, having retired impregnably behind the bolts and bars of his own house, and Jaffers was lying stunned in the parlour of the Coach and Horses. Great and strange ideas transcending experience often have less effect upon men and women than smaller, more tangible considerations. Iping was gay with bunting, and everybody was in gala dress. Whit Monday had been looked forward to for a month or more. By the afternoon even those who believed in the Unseen were beginning to resume their little amusements in a tentative fashion, on the supposition that he had quite gone away, and with the sceptics he was already a jest. But people, sceptics and believers alike, were remarkably sociable all that day.

Haysman's meadow was gay with a tent, in which Mrs Bunting and other ladies were preparing tea, while, without, the Sunday-school children ran races and played games under the noisy guidance of the curate and the Misses Cuss and

Sackbut. No doubt there was a slight uneasiness in the air, but people for the most part had the sense to conceal whatever imaginative qualms they experienced. On the village green an inclined string, down which, clinging the while to a pulley-swung handle, one could be hurled violently against a sack at the other end, came in for considerable favour among the adolescent. There were swings and coconut shies and prom-enading, and the steam organ attached to the swings filled the air with a pungent flavour of oil and with equally pungent music. Members of the Club, who had attended church in the morning, were splendid in badges of pink and green, and some of the gayer-minded had also adorned their bowler hats with brilliant-coloured favours of ribbon. Old Fletcher, whose conceptions of holiday-making were severe, was visible through the jasmine about his window or through the open door (whichever way you chose to look), poised delicately on a plank supported on two chairs and whitewashing the ceiling of his front room.

About four o'clock a stranger entered the village from the direction of the downs. He was a short, stout person in an extraordinarily shabby top hat, and he appeared to be very much out of breath. His cheeks were alternately limp and tightly puffed. His mottled face was apprehensive, and he moved with a sort of reluctant alacrity. He turned the corner by the church and directed his way to the Coach and Horses. Among others old Fletcher remembers seeing him, and indeed the old gentleman was so struck by his peculiar agitation that he inadvertently allowed a quantity of whitewash to run down the brush into the sleeve of his coat while regarding him.

This stranger, to the perceptions of the proprietor of the coconut shy, appeared to be talking to himself, and Mr Huxter remarked the same thing. He stopped at the foot of the Coach and Horses steps, and, according to Mr Huxter, appeared to undergo a severe internal struggle before he could induce himself to enter the house. Finally he marched up the steps, and was seen by Mr Huxter to turn to the left and open the door of the parlour. Mr Huxter heard voices from within the room and from the bar apprising the man of his error. "That room's private!" said Hall, and the stranger shut the door clumsily and went into the bar.

In the course of a few minutes he reappeared, wiping his lips with the back of his hand with an air of quiet satisfaction that somehow impressed Mr Huxter as assumed. He stood looking about him for some moments, and then Mr Huxter saw him walk in an oddly furtive manner towards the gates of the yard, upon which the parlour window opened. The stranger, after some hesitation, leant against one of the gateposts, produced a short clay pipe and prepared to fill it. His fingers trembled while doing so. He lit it clumsily and, folding his arms, began to smoke in a languid attitude, an attitude which his occasional quick glances up the yard altogether belied.

All this Mr Huxter saw over the canisters of the tobacco window, and the singularity of the man's behaviour prompted him to maintain his observation.

Presently the stranger stood up abruptly and put his pipe in his pocket. Then he vanished into the yard. Forthwith Mr Huxter, conceiving he was witness of some petty larceny, leapt round his counter and ran out into the road to intercept the thief. As he did so, Mr Marvel reappeared, his hat askew, a big bundle in a blue tablecloth in one hand and three books tied together – as it proved afterwards with the vicar's braces – in the other. Directly he saw Huxter he gave a sort of gasp, and turning sharply to the left, began to run. "Stop thief!" cried Huxter, and set off after him.

Mr Huxter's sensations were vivid but brief. He saw the man just before him and spurting briskly for the church corner and the down road. He saw the village flags and festivities beyond, and a face or two turned towards him. He bawled "Stop thief!" again, and set off gallantly. He had hardly gone ten strides before his shin was caught in some mysterious fashion, and he was no longer running, but flying with incredible velocity through the air. He saw the ground suddenly close to his head. The world seemed to splash into a million whirling specks of light, and "subsequent proceedings interested him no more".*

11

In the Coach and Horses

NOW IN ORDER CLEARLY to understand what had
happened in the inn, it is necessary to go back to the
moment when Mr Marvel first came into view of Mr Huxter's
window. At that precise moment Mr Cuss and Mr Bunting
were in the parlour. They were seriously investigating the
strange occurrences of the morning, and were, with Mr Hall's
permission, making a thorough examination of the Invisible
Man's belongings. Jaffers had partially recovered from his
fall and had gone home in the charge of his sympathetic
friends. The stranger's scattered garments had been removed
by Mrs Hall and the room tidied up. And on the table under
the window where the stranger had been wont to work, Cuss
had hit almost at once on three big books in manuscript
labelled "Diary".

"Diary!" said Cuss, putting the three books on the table.
"Now, at any rate, we shall learn something." The vicar stood
with his hands on the table.

"Diary," repeated Cuss, sitting down, putting two volumes
to support the third and opening it. "H'm – no name on the
flyleaf. Bother! – cipher. And figures."

The vicar came round to look over his shoulder.

Cuss turned the pages over with a face suddenly disappointed.
"I'm – dear me! It's all cipher, Bunting."

"There are no diagrams?" asked Mr Bunting. "No illustrations throwing light—"

"See for yourself," said Mr Cuss. "Some of it's mathematical and some of it's Russian or some such language (to judge by the letters), and some of it's Greek. Now the Greek I thought *you*—"

"Of course," said Mr Bunting, taking out and wiping his spectacles and feeling suddenly very uncomfortable – for he had no Greek left in his mind worth talking about. "Yes – the Greek, of course, may furnish a clue."

"I'll find you a place."

"I'd rather glance through the volumes first," said Mr Bunting, still wiping. "A general impression first, Cuss, and *then*, you know, we can go looking for clues."

He coughed, put on his glasses, arranged them fastidiously, coughed again and wished something would happen to avert the seemingly inevitable exposure. Then he took the volume Cuss handed him in a leisurely manner. And then something did happen.

The door opened suddenly.

Both gentlemen started violently, looked round and were relieved to see a sporadically rosy face beneath a furry silk hat. "Tap?"* asked the face, and stood staring.

"No," said both gentlemen at once.

"Over the other side, my man," said Mr Bunting. And "Please shut that door," said Mr Cuss irritably.

"All right," said the intruder, as it seemed, in a low voice curiously different from the huskiness of its first enquiry. "Right you are," said the intruder in the former voice. "Stand clear!" and he vanished and closed the door.

"A sailor, I should judge," said Mr Bunting. "Amusing fellows they are. 'Stand clear!' indeed. A nautical term referring to his getting back out of the room, I suppose."

CHAPTER 11

"I dare say so," said Cuss. "My nerves are all loose today. It quite made me jump – the door opening like that."

Mr Bunting smiled as if he had not jumped. "And now," he said with a sigh, "these books."

"One minute," said Cuss, and went and locked the door. "Now I think we are safe from interruption."

Someone sniffed as he did so.

"One thing is indisputable," said Bunting, drawing up a chair next to that of Cuss. "There certainly have been very strange things happen in Iping during the last few days – very strange. I cannot of course believe in this absurd invisibility story—"

"It's incredible," said Cuss, "incredible. But the fact remains that I saw... I certainly saw right down his sleeve—"

"But did you... are you sure? Suppose a mirror for instance – hallucinations are so easily produced. I don't know if you have ever seen a really good conjuror—"

"I won't argue again," said Cuss. "We've thrashed that out, Bunting. And just now there's these books – ah! Here's some of what I take to be Greek! Greek letters certainly."

He pointed to the middle of the page. Mr Bunting flushed slightly and brought his face nearer, apparently finding some difficulty with his glasses. Suddenly he became aware of a strange feeling at the nape of his neck. He tried to raise his head, and encountered an immovable resistance. The feeling was a curious pressure, the grip of a heavy, firm hand, and it bore his chin irresistibly to the table. "*Don't move, little men,*" whispered a voice, "*or I'll brain you both!*" He looked into the face of Cuss, close to his own, and each saw a horrified reflection of his own sickly astonishment.

"I'm sorry to handle you roughly," said the Voice, "but it's unavoidable.

"Since when did you learn to pry into an investigator's private memoranda?" said the Voice; and two chins struck the table simultaneously, and two sets of teeth rattled.

"Since when did you learn to invade the private rooms of a man in misfortune?" And the concussion was repeated.

"Where have they put my clothes?

"Listen," said the Voice. "The windows are fastened and I've taken the key out of the door. I am a fairly strong man, and I have the poker handy – besides being invisible. There's not the slightest doubt that I could kill you both and get away quite easily if I wanted to – do you understand? Very well. If I let you go will you promise not to try any nonsense and do what I tell you?"

The vicar and the doctor looked at one another, and the doctor pulled a face. "Yes," said Mr Bunting, and the doctor repeated it. Then the pressure on the necks relaxed, and the doctor and the vicar sat up, both very red in the face and wriggling their heads.

"Please keep sitting where you are," said the Invisible Man. "Here's the poker, you see.

"When I came into this room," continued the Invisible Man, after presenting the poker to the tip of the nose of each of his visitors, "I did not expect to find it occupied, and I expected to find, in addition to my books of memoranda, an outfit of clothing. Where is it? No – don't rise. I can see it's gone. Now, just at present, though the days are quite warm enough for an invisible man to run about stark, the evenings are chilly. I want clothing – and other accommodation – and I must also have those three books."

12

The Invisible Man Loses His Temper

IT IS UNAVOIDABLE THAT at this point the narrative should break off again, for a certain very painful reason that will presently be apparent. While these things were going on in the parlour, and while Mr Huxter was watching Mr Marvel smoking his pipe against the gate, not a dozen yards away were Mr Hall and Teddy Henfrey discussing in a state of cloudy puzzlement the one Iping topic.

Suddenly there came a violent thud against the door of the parlour, a sharp cry, and then – silence.

"*Hul* – lo!" said Teddy Henfrey.

"Hul – *lo*!" from the tap.

Mr Hall took things in slowly but surely. "That ain't right," he said, and came round from behind the bar towards the parlour door.

He and Teddy approached the door together, with intent faces. Their eyes considered. "Summat wrong," said Hall, and Henfrey nodded agreement. Whiffs of an unpleasant chemical odour met them, and there was a muffled sound of conversation, very rapid and subdued.

"You all raight thur?" asked Hall, rapping.

The muttered conversation ceased abruptly, for a moment silence, then the conversation was resumed in hissing whispers, then a sharp cry of "No! No, you don't!" There came a sudden motion and the oversetting of a chair, a brief struggle. Silence again.

"What the dooce?" exclaimed Henfrey, *sotto voce*.

"You – all – raight – thur?" asked Mr Hall sharply, again.

The vicar's voice answered with a curious jerking intonation: "Quire ri – ight. Please don't – interrupt."

"Odd!" said Mr Henfrey.

"Odd!" said Mr Hall.

"Says, 'Don't interrupt,'" said Henfrey.

"I heerd 'n," said Hall.

"And a sniff," said Henfrey.

They remained listening. The conversation was rapid and subdued. "I *can't*," said Mr Bunting, his voice rising. "I tell you, sir, I *will* not."

"What was that?" asked Henfrey.

"Says he wi' nart," said Hall. "Warn't speakin' to us, wuz he?"

"Disgraceful!" said Mr Bunting within.

"'Disgraceful',", said Mr Henfrey. "I heard it – *distinct*.

"Who's that speaking now?" asked Henfrey.

"Mr Cuss, I s'pose," said Hall. "Can you hear – anything?"

Silence. The sounds within indistinct and perplexing.

"Sounds like throwing the tablecloth about," said Hall.

Mrs Hall appeared behind the bar. Hall made gestures of silence and invitation. This roused Mrs Hall's wifely opposition. "What yer listenin' there for, Hall?" she asked. "Ain't you nothin' better to do – busy day like this?"

Hall tried to convey everything by grimaces and dumb show, but Mrs Hall was obdurate. She raised her voice. So Hall and Henfrey, rather crestfallen, tiptoed back to the bar, gesticulating to explain to her.

At first she refused to see anything in what they had heard at all. Then she insisted on Hall keeping silence, while Henfrey told her his story. She was inclined to think the whole business nonsense – perhaps they were just moving the furniture about.

"I heerd 'n say 'disgraceful'; *that* I did," said Hall.

"*I* heerd that, Mis' Hall," said Henfrey.

"Like as not—" began Mrs Hall.

"Hsh!" said Mr Teddy Henfrey. "Didn't I hear the window?"

"What window?" asked Mrs Hall.

"Parlour window," said Henfrey.

Everyone stood listening intently. Mrs Hall's eyes, directed straight before her, saw without seeing the brilliant oblong of the inn door, the road white and vivid, and Huxter's shopfront blistering in the June sun. Abruptly Huxter's door opened and Huxter appeared, eyes staring with excitement, arms gesticulating. "*Yap!*" cried Huxter. "Stop thief!" and he ran obliquely across the oblong towards the yard gates, and vanished.

Simultaneously came a tumult from the parlour, and a sound of windows being closed.

Hall, Henfrey and the human contents of the tap rushed out at once pell-mell into the street. They saw someone whisk round the corner towards the down road, and Mr Huxter executing a complicated leap in the air that ended on his face and shoulder. Down the street people were standing astonished or running towards them.

Mr Huxter was stunned. Henfrey stopped to discover this, but Hall and the two labourers from the tap rushed at once to the corner, shouting incoherent things, and saw Mr Marvel vanishing by the corner of the church wall. They appear to have jumped to the impossible conclusion that this was the Invisible Man suddenly become visible, and set off at once along the lane in pursuit. But Hall had hardly run a dozen yards before he gave a loud shout of astonishment and went flying headlong sideways, clutching one of the labourers and bringing him to the ground. He had been charged just as one charges a man at football. The second labourer came round in a circle, stared and, conceiving that Hall had tumbled over of his own accord, turned to resume the pursuit, only to be tripped by the ankle just as Huxter had been. Then, as the first labourer struggled to his feet, he was kicked sideways by a blow that might have felled an ox.

As he went down, the rush from the direction of the village green came round the corner. The first to appear was the proprietor of the coconut shy, a burly man in a blue jersey. He was astonished to see the lane empty save for three men sprawling absurdly on the ground. And then something happened to his rearmost foot, and he went headlong and rolled sideways just in time to graze the feet of his brother and partner, following headlong. The two were then kicked, knelt on, fallen over and cursed by quite a number of over-hasty people.

Now when Hall and Henfrey and the labourers ran out of the house, Mrs Hall, who had been disciplined by years of experience, remained in the bar next the till. And suddenly the parlour door was opened, and Mr Cuss appeared and, without glancing at her, rushed at once down the steps towards the corner. "Hold him!" he cried. "Don't let him drop that parcel! You can see him so long as he holds the parcel." He knew nothing of the existence of Marvel. For the Invisible Man had handed over the books and bundle in the yard. The face of Mr Cuss was angry and resolute, but his costume was defective, a sort of limp white kilt that could only have passed muster in Greece. "Hold him!" he bawled. "He's got my trousers! And every stitch of the vicar's clothes!

"'Tend to him in a minute!" he cried to Henfrey as he passed the prostrate Huxter and, coming round the corner to join the tumult, was promptly knocked off his feet into an indecorous sprawl. Somebody in full flight trod heavily on his finger. He yelled, struggled to regain his feet, was knocked against and thrown on all fours again, and became aware that he was involved not in a capture, but a rout. Everyone was running back to the village. He rose again and was hit severely behind the ear. He staggered and set off back to the Coach and Horses forthwith, leaping over the deserted Huxter, who was now sitting up, on his way.

Behind him as he was halfway up the inn steps he heard a sudden yell of rage, rising sharply out of the confusion of cries, and a sounding smack in someone's face. He recognized the voice as that of the Invisible Man, and the note was that of a man suddenly infuriated by a painful blow.

In another moment Mr Cuss was back in the parlour. "He's coming back, Bunting!" he said, rushing in. "Save yourself! He's gone mad!"

Mr Bunting was standing in the window engaged in an attempt to clothe himself in the hearthrug and a *West Surrey Gazette*. "Who's coming?" he said, so startled that his costume narrowly escaped disintegration.

"Invisible Man," said Cuss, and rushed to the window. "We'd better clear out from here! He's fighting mad! Mad!"

In another moment he was out in the yard.

"Good Heavens!" said Mr Bunting, hesitating between two horrible alternatives. He heard a frightful struggle in the passage of the inn, and his decision was made. He clambered out of the window, adjusted his costume hastily, and fled up the village as fast as his fat little legs would carry him.

From the moment when the Invisible Man screamed with rage and Mr Bunting made his memorable flight up the village, it became impossible to give a consecutive account of affairs in Iping. Possibly the Invisible Man's original intention was simply to cover Marvel's retreat with the clothes and books. But his temper, at no time very good, seems to have gone completely at some chance blow, and forthwith he set to smiting and overthrowing, for the mere satisfaction of hurting.

You must figure the street full of running figures, of doors slamming and fights for hiding places. You must figure the tumult suddenly striking on the unstable equilibrium of old Fletcher's planks and two chairs – with cataclysmal results. You must figure an appalled couple caught dismally in a swing. And then the whole tumultuous rush has passed and the Iping street with its gauds and flags is deserted save for the still-raging Unseen, and littered with coconuts, overthrown canvas screens and the scattered stock-in-trade of a sweetstuff stall. Everywhere there is a sound of closing shutters and shooting bolts, and the only visible humanity is an occasional flitting eye under a raised eyebrow in the corner of a window pane.

The Invisible Man amused himself for a little while by breaking all the windows in the Coach and Horses, and then he thrust a street lamp through the parlour window of Mrs Gribble. He it must have been who cut the telegraph wire to Adderdean just beyond Higgins's cottage on the Adderdean road. And after that, as his peculiar qualities allowed, he passed out of human perceptions altogether, and he was neither heard, seen nor felt in Iping any more. He vanished absolutely.

But it was the best part of two hours before any human being ventured out again into the desolation of Iping Street.

13

Mr Marvel Discusses His Resignation

WHEN THE DUSK WAS GATHERING and Iping was just beginning to peep timorously forth again upon the shattered wreckage of its Bank Holiday, a short, thickset man in a shabby silk hat was marching painfully through the twilight behind the beechwoods on the road to Bramblehurst. He carried three books bound together by some sort of ornamental elastic ligature, and a bundle wrapped in a blue tablecloth. His rubicund face expressed consternation and fatigue; he appeared to be in a spasmodic sort of hurry. He was accompanied by a Voice other than his own, and ever and again he winced under the touch of unseen hands.

"If you give me the slip again," said the Voice, "if you attempt to give me the slip again…"

"Lord!" said Mr Marvel. "That shoulder's a mass of bruises as it is."

"…on my honour," said the Voice, "I will kill you."

"I didn't try to give you the slip," said Marvel, in a voice that was not far remote from tears. "I swear I didn't. I didn't know the blessed turning, that was all! How the devil was I to know the blessed turning? As it is, I've been knocked about—"

"You'll get knocked about a great deal more if you don't mind," said the Voice, and Mr Marvel abruptly became silent. He blew out his cheeks, and his eyes were eloquent of despair.

"It's bad enough to let these floundering yokels explode my little secret without *your* cutting off with my books. It's lucky for some of them they cut and ran when they did! Here am I – no one knew I was invisible! And now what am I to do?"

"What am *I* to do?" asked Marvel, *sotto voce*.

"It's all about. It will be in the papers! Everybody will be looking for me; everyone on their guard…" The Voice broke off into vivid curses and ceased.

The despair of Mr Marvel's face deepened, and his pace slackened.

"Go on!" said the Voice.

Mr Marvel's face assumed a greyish tint between the ruddier patches.

"Don't drop those books, stupid," said the Voice sharply – overtaking him.

"The fact is," said the Voice, "I shall have to make use of you. You're a poor tool, but I must."

"I'm a *miserable* tool," said Marvel.

"You are," said the Voice.

"I'm the worst possible tool you could have," said Marvel.

"I'm not strong," he said after a discouraging silence.

"I'm not over strong," he repeated.

"No?"

"And my heart's weak. That little business – I pulled it through, of course – but bless you! I could have dropped."

"Well?"

"I haven't the nerve and strength for the sort of thing you want."

"*I'll* stimulate you."

"I wish you wouldn't. I wouldn't like to mess up your plans, you know. But I might – out of sheer funk and misery."

CHAPTER 13

"You'd better not," said the Voice, with quiet emphasis.

"I wish I was dead," said Marvel.

"It ain't justice," he said. "You must admit – it seems to me I've a perfect right—"

"*Get* on!" said the Voice.

Mr Marvel mended his pace, and for a time they went in silence again.

"It's devilish hard," said Mr Marvel.

This was quite ineffectual. He tried another tack.

"What do I make by it?" he began again in a tone of unendurable wrong.

"Oh! *Shut up!*" said the Voice, with sudden amazing vigour. "I'll see to you all right. You do what you're told. You'll do it all right. You're a fool and all that, but you'll do—"

"I tell you, sir, I'm not the man for it. Respectfully – but it is so—"

"If you don't shut up I shall twist your wrist again," said the Invisible Man. "I want to think."

Presently two oblongs of yellow light appeared through the trees, and the square tower of a church loomed through the gloaming. "I shall keep my hand on your shoulder," said the Voice, "all through the village. Go straight through and try no foolery. It will be the worse for you if you do."

"I know that," sighed Mr Marvel. "I know all that."

The unhappy-looking figure in the obsolete silk hat passed up the street of the little village with his burdens, and vanished into the gathering darkness beyond the lights of the windows.

14

At Port Stowe

TEN O'CLOCK THE NEXT MORNING found Mr Marvel, unshaven, dirty and travel-stained, sitting with the books beside him and his hands deep in his pockets, looking very weary, nervous and uncomfortable and inflating his cheeks at frequent intervals, on the bench outside a little inn on the outskirts of Port Stowe. Beside him were the books, but now they were tied with string. The bundle had been abandoned in the pinewoods beyond Bramblehurst, in accordance with a change in the plans of the Invisible Man. Mr Marvel sat on the bench, and although no one took the slightest notice of him, his agitation remained at fever heat. His hands would go ever and again to his various pockets with a curious nervous fumbling.

When he had been sitting for the best part of an hour however, an elderly mariner, carrying a newspaper, came out of the inn and sat down beside him. "Pleasant day," said the mariner.

Mr Marvel glanced about him with something very like terror. "Very," he said.

"Just seasonable weather for the time of year," said the mariner, taking no denial.

"Quite," said Mr Marvel.

The mariner produced a toothpick, and (saving his regard) was engrossed thereby for some minutes. His eyes meanwhile were at liberty to examine Mr Marvel's dusty figure and the books beside him. As he had approached Mr Marvel he had heard a sound like the dropping of coins into a pocket. He was struck by the contrast of Mr Marvel's appearance with this suggestion of opulence. Thence his mind wandered back again to a topic that had taken a curiously firm hold of his imagination.

"Books?" he said suddenly, noisily finishing with the toothpick.

Mr Marvel started and looked at them. "Oh, yes," he said. "Yes, they're books."

"There's some extraordinary things in books," said the mariner.

"I believe you," said Mr Marvel.

"And some extraordinary things out of 'em," said the mariner.

"True likewise," said Mr Marvel. He eyed his interlocutor, and then glanced about him.

"There's some extraordinary things in newspapers, for example," said the mariner.

"There are."

"In *this* newspaper," said the mariner.

"Ah!" said Mr Marvel.

"There's a story," said the mariner, fixing Mr Marvel with an eye that was firm and deliberate, "there's a story about an invisible man, for instance."

Mr Marvel pulled his mouth askew and scratched his cheek and felt his ears glowing. "What will they be writing next?" he asked faintly. "Ostria, or America?"

"Neither," said the mariner. "*Here!*"

"Lord!" said Mr Marvel, starting.

"When I say *here*," said the mariner, to Mr Marvel's intense relief, "I don't of course mean here in this place – I mean hereabouts."

"An invisible man!" said Mr Marvel. "And what's *he* been up to?"

"Everything," said the mariner, controlling Marvel with his eye, and then amplifying: "Every Blessed Thing."

"I ain't seen a paper these four days," said Marvel.

"Iping's the place he started at," said the mariner.

"In-*deed*!" said Mr Marvel.

"He started there. And where he came from, nobody don't seem to know. Here it is: 'Peculiar Story from Iping'. And it says in this paper that the evidence is extraordinary strong – extraordinary."

"Lord!" said Mr Marvel.

"But then, it's a extraordinary story. There is a clergyman and a medical gent witnesses – saw 'im all right and proper – or leastways, didn't see 'im. He was staying, it says, at the Coach an' Horses, and no one don't seem to have been aware of his misfortune, it says, aware of his misfortune, until in an Alteration* in the inn, it says, his bandages on his head was torn off. It was then observed that his head was invisible. Attempts were At Once made to secure him, but casting off his garments, it says, he succeeded in escaping, but not until after a desperate struggle, In Which he had inflicted serious injuries, it says, on our worthy and able constable, Mr J.A. Jaffers. Pretty straight story, eh? Names and everything."

"Lord!" said Mr Marvel, looking nervously about him, trying to count the money in his pockets by his unaided sense of touch and full of a strange and novel idea. "It sounds most astonishing."

"Don't it? Extraordinary, *I* call it. Never heard tell of invisible men before, I haven't, but nowadays one hears such a lot of extraordinary things – that—"

"That all he did?" asked Marvel, trying to seem at his ease.

"It's enough, ain't it?" said the mariner.

"Didn't go back by any chance?" asked Marvel. "Just escaped and that's all, eh?"

"All!" said the mariner. "Why! Ain't it enough?"

"Quite enough," said Marvel.

"I should think it was enough," said the mariner. "I should think it was enough."

"He didn't have any pals – it don't say he had any pals, does it?" asked Mr Marvel, anxious.

"Ain't one of a sort enough for you?" asked the mariner. "No, thank Heaven, as one might say, he didn't."

He nodded his head slowly. "It makes me regular uncomfortable, the bare thought of that chap running about the country! He is at present At Large, and from certain evidence it is supposed that he has – taken – *took*, I suppose they mean – the road to Port Stowe. You see we're right *in* it! None of your American wonders, this time. And just think of the things he might do! Where'd you be, if he took a drop over and above, and had a fancy to go for you? Suppose he wants to rob – who can prevent him? He can trespass, he can burgle, he could walk through a cordon of policemen as easy as me or you could give the slip to a blind man! Easier! For these here blind chaps hear uncommon sharp, I'm told. And wherever there was liquor he fancied—"

"He's got a tremenjous advantage, certainly," said Mr Marvel. "And – well."

"You're right," said the mariner. "He *has*."

All this time Mr Marvel had been glancing about him intently, listening for faint footfalls, trying to detect imperceptible movements. He seemed on the point of some great resolution. He coughed behind his hand.

He looked about him again, listened, bent towards the mariner and lowered his voice: "The fact of it is – I happen – to know just a thing or two about this Invisible Man. From private sources."

"Oh!" said the mariner, interested. "*You?*"

"Yes," said Mr Marvel. "Me."

"Indeed!" said the mariner. "And may I ask—"

"You'll be astonished," said Mr Marvel behind his hand. "It's tremenjous."

"Indeed!" said the mariner.

"The fact is," began Mr Marvel eagerly in a confidential undertone. Suddenly his expression changed marvellously. "Ow!" he said. He rose stiffly in his seat. His face was eloquent of physical suffering. "Wow!" he said.

"What's up?" said the mariner, concerned.

"Toothache," said Mr Marvel, and put his hand to his ear. He caught hold of his books. "I must be getting on, I think," he said. He edged in a curious way along the seat away from his interlocutor.

"But you was just a-going to tell me about this here Invisible Man!" protested the mariner.

Mr Marvel seemed to consult with himself.

"Hoax," said a voice.

"It's a hoax," said Mr Marvel.

"But it's in the paper," said the mariner.

"Hoax all the same," said Marvel. "I know the chap that started the lie. There ain't no Invisible Man whatsoever – blimey."

"But how 'bout this paper? D'you mean to say—"

"Not a word of it," said Marvel stoutly.

The mariner stared, paper in hand. Mr Marvel jerkily faced about. "Wait a bit," said the mariner, rising and speaking slowly. "D'you mean to say—"

"I do," said Mr Marvel.

"Then why did you let me go on and tell you all this blarsted stuff, then? What d'yer mean by letting a man make a fool of himself like that for? Eh?"

Mr Marvel blew out his cheeks. The mariner was suddenly very red indeed; he clenched his hands. "I been talking here this ten minutes," he said, "and you, you little pot-bellied, leathery-faced son of an old boot, couldn't have the elementary manners—"

"Don't you come bandying words with *me*," said Mr Marvel.

"Bandying words! I'm a jolly good mind—"

"Come up," said a voice, and Mr Marvel was suddenly whirled about and started marching off in a curious spasmodic manner. "You'd better move on," said the mariner. "*Who's* moving on?" said Mr Marvel. He was receding obliquely with a curious hurrying gait, with occasional violent jerks forward. Some way along the road he began a muttered monologue, protests and recriminations.

"Silly devil!" said the mariner, legs wide apart, elbows akimbo, watching the receding figure. "I'll show you, you silly ass – hoaxing *me*! It's here in the paper!"

Mr Marvel retorted incoherently and, receding, was hidden by a bend in the road, but the mariner still stood magnificent in the midst of the way, until the approach of a butcher's cart dislodged him. Then he turned himself towards Port Stowe. "Full of extraordinary asses," he said softly to himself. "Just to take me down a bit – that was his silly game – it's on the paper!"

And there was another extraordinary thing he was presently to hear, that had happened quite close to him. And that was a vision of a "fist full of money" (no less) travelling without visible agency, along by the wall at the corner of St Michael's

Lane. A brother mariner had seen this wonderful sight that very morning. He had snatched at the money forthwith and had been knocked headlong, and when he had got to his feet the butterfly money had vanished. Our mariner was in the mood to believe anything, he declared, but that was a bit *too* stiff. Afterwards, however, he began to think things over.

The story of the flying money was true. And all about that neighbourhood, even from the august London and County Banking Company, from the tills of shops and inns – doors standing that sunny weather entirely open – money had been quietly and dextrously making off that day in handfuls and rouleaux, floating quietly along by walls and shady places, dodging quickly from the approaching eyes of men. And it had, though no man had traced it, invariably ended its mysterious flight in the pocket of that agitated gentleman in the obsolete silk hat, sitting outside the little inn on the outskirts of Port Stowe.

It was ten days after – and indeed only when the Burdock story was already old – that the mariner collated these facts and began to understand how near he had been to the Wonderful Invisible Man.

15

The Man Who Was Running

I N THE EARLY EVENING TIME Dr Kemp was sitting in his study in the belvedere on the hill overlooking Burdock. It was a pleasant little room, with three windows – north, west and south – and bookshelves crowded with books and scientific publications, and a broad writing table, and, under the north window, a microscope, glass slips, minute instruments, some cultures and scattered bottles of reagents. Dr Kemp's solar lamp was lit, albeit the sky was still bright with the sunset light, and his blinds were up because there was no offence of peering outsiders to require them pulled down. Dr Kemp was a tall and slender young man, with flaxen hair and a moustache almost white, and the work he was upon would earn him, he hoped, the fellowship of the Royal Society,* so highly did he think of it.

And his eye presently wandering from his work caught the sunset blazing at the back of the hill that is over against his own. For a minute perhaps he sat, pen in mouth, admiring the rich golden colour above the crest, and then his attention was attracted by the little figure of a man, inky black, running over the hill brow towards him. He was a shortish little man, and he wore a high hat, and he was running so fast that his legs verily twinkled.

"Another of those fools," said Dr Kemp. "Like that ass who ran into me this morning round a corner, with his ''Visible

Man a-coming, sir!' I can't imagine what possesses people. One might think we were in the thirteenth century."

He got up, went to the window and stared at the dusky hillside and the dark little figure tearing down it. "He seems in a confounded hurry," said Dr Kemp, "but be doesn't seem to be getting on. If his pockets were full of lead, he couldn't run heavier.

"Spurted, sir," said Dr Kemp.

In another moment the higher of the villas that had clambered up the hill from Burdock had occulted the running figure. He was visible again for a moment, and again, and then again, three times between the three detached houses that came next, and then the terrace hid him.

"Asses!" said Dr Kemp, swinging round on his heel and walking back to his writing table.

But those who saw the fugitive nearer and perceived the abject terror on his perspiring face, being themselves in the open roadway, did not share in the doctor's contempt. By the man pounded, and as he ran he chinked like a well-filled purse that is tossed to and fro. He looked neither to the right nor the left, but his dilated eyes stared straight downhill to where the lamps were being lit, and the people were crowded in the street. And his ill-shaped mouth fell apart, and a glairy* foam lay on his lips, and his breath came hoarse and noisy. All he passed stopped and began staring up the road and down, and interrogating one another with an inkling of discomfort for the reason of his haste.

And then presently, far up the hill, a dog playing in the road yelped and ran under a gate, and as they still wondered something – a wind – a pad, pad, pad – a sound like a panting breathing – rushed by.

CHAPTER 15

People screamed. People sprang off the pavement. It passed in shouts, it passed by instinct down the hill. They were shouting in the street before Marvel was halfway there. They were bolting into houses and slamming the doors behind them with the news. He heard it and made one last desperate spurt. Fear came striding by, rushed ahead of him and in a moment had seized the town.

"The Invisible Man is coming! *The Invisible Man!*"

16

In the Jolly Cricketers

THE JOLLY CRICKETERS is just at the bottom of the hill, where the tramlines begin. The barman leant his fat red arms on the counter and talked of horses with an anaemic cabman, while a black-bearded man in grey snapped up biscuit and cheese, drank Burton,* and conversed in American with a policeman off duty.

"What's the shouting about?" said the anaemic cabman going off at a tangent, trying to see up the hill over the dirty yellow blind in the low window of the inn. Somebody ran by outside. "Fire, perhaps," said the barman.

Footsteps approached, running heavily, the door was pushed open violently and Marvel, weeping and dishevelled, his hat gone, the neck of his coat torn open, rushed in, made a convulsive turn and attempted to shut the door. It was held half open by a strap.

"Coming!" he bawled, his voice shrieking with terror. "He's coming. The 'Visible Man! After me! For Gawd's sake! 'Elp! 'Elp! 'Elp!"

"Shut the doors," said the policeman. "Who's coming? What's the row?" He went to the door, released the strap, and it slammed. The American closed the other door.

"Lemme go inside," said Marvel, staggering and weeping, but still clutching the books. "Lemme go inside. Lock me in

– somewhere. I tell you he's after me. I give him the slip. He said he'd kill me and he will."

"*You're* safe," said the man with the black beard. "The door's shut. What's it all about?"

"Lemme go inside," said Marvel, and shrieked aloud as a blow suddenly made the fastened door shiver and was followed by a hurried rapping and a shouting outside.

"Hullo," cried the policeman, "who's there?"

Mr Marvel began to make frantic dives at panels that looked like doors. "He'll kill me – he's got a knife or something. For Gawd's sake!"

"Here you are," said the barman. "Come in here." And he held up the flap of the bar.

Mr Marvel rushed behind the bar as the summons outside was repeated. "Don't open the door," he screamed. "*Please* don't open the door. *Where* shall I hide?"

"This, this Invisible Man, then?" asked the man with the black beard, with one hand behind him. "I guess it's about time we saw him."

The window of the inn was suddenly smashed in, and there was a screaming and running to and fro in the street. The policeman had been standing on the settee staring out, craning to see who was at the door. He got down with raised eyebrows. "It's that," he said. The barman stood in front of the bar-parlour door which was now locked on Mr Marvel, stared at the smashed window, and came round to the two other men.

Everything was suddenly quiet. "I wish I had my truncheon," said the policeman, going irresolutely to the door. "Once we open, in he comes. There's no stopping him."

"Don't you be in too much hurry about that door," said the anaemic cabman anxiously.

"Draw the bolts," said the man with the black beard, "and if he comes…" He showed a revolver in his hand.

"That won't do," said the policeman. "That's murder."

"I know what country I'm in," said the man with the beard. "I'm going to let off at his legs. Draw the bolts."

"Not with that thing going off behind me," said the barman, craning over the blind.

"Very well," said the man with the black beard, and stooping down, revolver ready, drew them himself. Barman, cabman and policeman faced about.

"Come in," said the bearded man in an undertone, standing back and facing the unbolted doors with his pistol behind him. No one came in, the door remained closed. Five minutes afterwards when a second cabman pushed his head in cautiously, they were still waiting, and an anxious face peered out of the bar parlour and supplied information. "Are all the doors of the house shut?" asked Marvel. "He's going round – prowling round. He's as artful as the devil."

"Good Lord!" said the burly barman. "There's the back! Just watch them doors! I say!" He looked about him helplessly. The bar-parlour door slammed and they heard the key turn. "There's the yard door and the private door. The yard door—"

He rushed out of the bar.

In a minute he reappeared with a carving knife in his hand. "The yard door was open!" he said, and his fat underlip dropped. "He may be in the house now!" said the first cabman.

"He's not in the kitchen," said the barman. "There's two women there, and I've stabbed every inch of it with this little beef slicer. And they don't think he's come in. They haven't noticed—"

"Have you fastened it?" asked the first cabman.

"I'm out of frocks,"* said the barman.

The man with the beard replaced his revolver. And even as he did so the flap of the bar was shut down and the bolt clicked, and then with a tremendous thud the catch of the door snapped and the bar-parlour door burst open. They heard Marvel squeal like a caught leveret,* and forthwith they were clambering over the bar to his rescue. The bearded man's revolver cracked and the looking glass at the back of the parlour was starred brightly and came smashing and tinkling down.

As the barman entered the room he saw Marvel, curiously crumpled up and struggling against the door that led to the yard and kitchen. The door flew open while the barman hesitated, and Marvel was dragged into the kitchen. There was a scream and a clatter of pans. Marvel, head down and lugging back obstinately, was forced to the kitchen door, and the bolts were drawn.

Then the policeman, who had been trying to pass the barman, rushed in, followed by one of the cabmen, gripped the wrist of the invisible hand that collared Marvel, was hit in the face and went reeling back. The door opened, and Marvel made a frantic effort to obtain a lodgement behind it. Then the cabman clutched something. "I got him," said the cabman. The barman's red hands came clawing at the Unseen. "Here he is!" said the barman.

Mr Marvel, released, suddenly dropped to the ground and made an attempt to crawl behind the legs of the fighting men. The struggle blundered round the edge of the door. The voice of the Invisible Man was heard for the first time, yelling out sharply, as the policeman trod on his foot. Then he cried out passionately and his fists flew round like flails. The cabman suddenly whooped and doubled up, kicked under the diaphragm.

The door into the bar parlour from the kitchen slammed and covered Mr Marvel's retreat. The men in the kitchen found themselves clutching at and struggling with empty air.

"Where's he gone?" cried the man with the beard. "Out?"

"This way," said the policeman, stepping into the yard and stopping.

A piece of tile whizzed by his head and smashed among the crockery on the kitchen table.

"I'll show him," shouted the man with the black beard, and suddenly a steel barrel shone over the policeman's shoulder, and five bullets had followed one another into the twilight whence the missile had come. As he fired, the man with the beard moved his hand in a horizontal curve, so that his shots radiated out into the narrow yard like spokes from a wheel.

A silence followed. "Five cartridges," said the man with the black beard. "That's the best of all. Four aces and the joker. Get a lantern, someone, and come and feel about for his body."

17

Dr Kemp's Visitor

D R KEMP HAD CONTINUED writing in his study until the shots aroused him. Crack, crack, crack, they came one after the other.

"Hullo!" said Dr Kemp, putting his pen into his mouth again and listening. "Who's letting off revolvers in Burdock? What are the asses at now?"

He went to the south window, threw it up and, leaning out, stared down on the network of windows, beaded gas lamps and shops with black interstices of roof and yard that made up the town at night. "Looks like a crowd down the hill," he said, "by the Cricketers," and remained watching. Thence his eyes wandered over the town to far away where the ships' lights shone and the pier glowed, a little illuminated pavilion like a gem of yellow light. The moon in its first quarter hung over the western hill, and the stars were clear and almost tropically bright.

After five minutes, during which his mind had travelled into a remote speculation of social conditions of the future, and lost itself at last over the time dimension, Dr Kemp roused himself with a sigh, pulled down the window again, and returned to his writing desk.

It must have been about an hour after this that the front doorbell rang. He had been writing slackly and with intervals of abstraction, since the shots. He sat listening. He heard the servant answer the door, and waited for her feet on the staircase, but she did not come. "Wonder what that was," said Dr Kemp.

He tried to resume his work, failed, got up, went downstairs from his study to the landing, rang and called over the balustrade to the housemaid as she appeared in the hall below. "Was that a letter?" he asked.

"Only a runaway ring, sir," she answered.

"I'm restless tonight," he said to himself. He went back to his study, and this time attacked his work resolutely. In a little while he was hard at work again, and the only sounds in the room were the ticking of the clock and the subdued shrillness of his quill, hurrying in the very centre of the circle of light his lampshade threw on his table.

It was two o'clock before Dr Kemp had finished his work for the night. He rose, yawned and went downstairs to bed. He had already removed his coat and vest, when he noticed that he was thirsty. He took a candle and went down to the dining room in search of a syphon and whisky.

Dr Kemp's scientific pursuits had made him a very observant man, and as he recrossed the hall, he noticed a dark spot on the linoleum near the mat at the foot of the stairs. He went on upstairs, and then it suddenly occurred to him to ask himself what the spot on the linoleum might be. Apparently some subconscious element was at work. At any rate, he turned with his burden, went back to the hall, put down the syphon and whisky and, bending down, touched the spot. Without any great surprise he found it had the stickiness and colour of drying blood.

He took up his burden again and returned upstairs, looking about him and trying to account for the blood spot. On the landing he saw something and stopped astonished. The door handle of his own room was bloodstained.

He looked at his own hand. It was quite clean, and then he remembered that the door of his room had been open when he came down from his study, and that consequently he had not touched the handle at all. He went straight into his room, his face quite calm – perhaps a trifle more resolute than usual. His glance, wandering inquisitively, fell on the bed. On the counterpane was a mess of blood, and the sheet had been torn. He had not noticed this before, because he had walked straight to the dressing table. On the further side the bedclothes were depressed as if someone had been recently sitting there.

Then he had an odd impression that he had heard a low voice say, "Good Heavens! – *Kemp!*" But Dr Kemp was no believer in voices.

He stood staring at the tumbled sheets. Was that really a voice? He looked about again, but noticed nothing further than the disordered and bloodstained bed. Then he distinctly heard a movement across the room, near the wash-hand stand. All men, however highly educated, retain some superstitious inklings. The feeling that is called "eerie" came upon him. He closed the door of the room, came forward to the dressing table and put down his burdens. Suddenly, with a start, he perceived a coiled and bloodstained bandage of linen rag hanging in mid-air, between him and the wash-hand stand.

He stared at this in amazement. It was an empty bandage, a bandage properly tied but quite empty. He would have advanced to grasp it, but a touch arrested him, and a voice speaking quite close to him.

"Kemp!" said the Voice.

"Eh?" said Kemp, with his mouth open.

"Keep your nerve," said the Voice. "I'm an invisible man."

Kemp made no answer for a space, simply stared at the bandage. "Invisible man," he said.

"I'm an invisible man," repeated the Voice.

The story he had been active to ridicule only that morning rushed through Kemp's brain. He does not appear to have been either very much frightened or very greatly surprised at the moment. Realization came later.

"I thought it was all a lie," he said. The thought uppermost in his mind was the reiterated arguments of the morning. "Have you a bandage on?" he asked.

"Yes," said the Invisible Man.

"Oh!" said Kemp, and then roused himself. "I say!" he said. "But this is nonsense. It's some trick." He stepped forward suddenly, and his hand, extended towards the bandage, met invisible fingers.

He recoiled at the touch and his colour changed.

"Keep steady, Kemp, for God's sake! I want help badly. Stop!"

The hand gripped his arm. He struck at it.

"Kemp!" cried the Voice. "Kemp! Keep steady!" and the grip tightened.

A frantic desire to free himself took possession of Kemp. The hand of the bandaged arm gripped his shoulder, and he was suddenly tripped and flung backwards upon the bed. He opened his mouth to shout, and the corner of the sheet was thrust between his teeth. The Invisible Man had him down grimly, but his arms were free and he struck and tried to kick savagely.

"Listen to reason, will you?" said the Invisible Man, sticking to him in spite of a pounding in the ribs. "By Heaven! You'll madden me in a minute!

"Lie still, you fool!" bawled the Invisible Man in Kemp's ear.

Kemp struggled for another moment and then lay still.

"If you shout I'll smash your face," said the Invisible Man, relieving his mouth.

"I'm an invisible man. It's no foolishness, and no magic. I really am an invisible man. And I want your help. I don't want to hurt you, but if you behave like a frantic rustic, I must. Don't you remember me, Kemp? Griffin, of University College?"

"Let me get up," said Kemp. "I'll stop where I am. And let me sit quiet for a minute."

He sat up and felt his neck.

"I am Griffin, of University College, and I have made myself invisible. I am just an ordinary man – a man you have known – made invisible."

"Griffin?" said Kemp.

"Griffin," answered the Voice – "a younger student than you were, almost an albino, six feet high, and broad, with a pink-and-white face and red eyes – who won the medal for chemistry."

"I am confused," said Kemp. "My brain is rioting. What has this to do with Griffin?"

"I *am* Griffin."

Kemp thought. "It's horrible," he said. "But what devilry must happen to make a man invisible?"

"It's no devilry. It's a process, sane and intelligible enough—"

"It's horrible!" said Kemp. "How on earth—"

"It's horrible enough. But I'm wounded and in pain, and tired – great God! Kemp, you are a man. Take it steady. Give me some food and drink, and let me sit down here."

Kemp stared at the bandage as it moved across the room, then saw a basket chair dragged across the floor and come to rest near the bed. It creaked, and the seat was depressed a quarter of an inch or so. He rubbed his eyes and felt his neck again. "This beats ghosts," he said, and laughed stupidly.

"That's better. Thank Heaven, you're getting sensible!"

"Or silly," said Kemp, and knuckled his eyes.

"Give me some whisky. I'm near dead."

"It didn't feel so. Where are you? If I get up shall I run into you? *There!* All right. Whisky? Here. Where shall I give it you?"

The chair creaked and Kemp felt the glass drawn away from him. He let go by an effort; his instinct was all against it. It came to rest poised twenty inches above the front edge of the seat of the chair. He stared at it in infinite perplexity. "This is – this *must* be – hypnotism. You must have suggested you are invisible."

"Nonsense," said the Voice.

"It's frantic."

"Listen to me."

"I demonstrated conclusively this morning," began Kemp, "that invisibility—"

"Never mind what you've demonstrated! I'm starving," said the Voice, "and the night is – chilly to a man without clothes."

"Food!" said Kemp.

The tumbler of whisky tilted itself. "Yes," said the Invisible Man rapping it down. "Have you got a dressing gown?"

Kemp made some exclamation in an undertone. He walked to a wardrobe and produced a robe of dingy scarlet. "This do?" he asked. It was taken from him. It hung limp for a moment in mid-air, fluttered weirdly, stood full and decorous buttoning itself and sat down in his chair. "Drawers, socks, slippers would be a comfort," said the Unseen curtly. "And food."

"Anything. But this is the insanest thing I ever was in in my life!"

He turned out his drawers for the articles, and then went downstairs to ransack his larder. He came back with some cold cutlets and bread, pulled up a light table and placed them before his guest. "Never mind knives," said his visitor, and a cutlet hung in mid-air, with a sound of gnawing.

"Invisible!" said Kemp, and sat down on a bedroom chair.

"I always like to get something about me before I eat," said the Invisible Man, with a full mouth, eating greedily. "Queer fancy!"

"I suppose that wrist is all right," said Kemp.

"Trust me," said the Invisible Man.

"Of *all* the strange and wonderful—"

"Exactly. But it's odd I should blunder into *your* house to get my bandaging. My first stroke of luck! Anyhow I meant to sleep in this house tonight. You must stand that! It's a filthy nuisance, my blood showing, isn't it? Quite a clot over there. Gets visible as it coagulates, I see. I've been in the house three hours."

"But how's it done?" began Kemp in a tone of exasperation. "Confound it! The whole business – it's unreasonable from beginning to end."

"Quite reasonable," said the Invisible Man. "Perfectly reasonable."

He reached over and secured the whisky bottle. Kemp stared at the devouring dressing gown. A ray of candlelight penetrating a torn patch in the right shoulder made a triangle of light under the left ribs. "What were the shots?" he asked. "How did the shooting begin?"

"There was a fool of a man – a sort of confederate of mine – curse him! – who tried to steal my money. *Has* done so."

"Is *he* invisible too?"

"No."

"Well?"

"Can't I have some more to eat before I tell you all that? I'm hungry – in pain. And you want me to tell stories!"

Kemp got up. "*You* didn't do any shooting?" he asked.

"Not me," said his visitor. "Some fool I'd never seen fired at random. A lot of them got seated. They all got scared at me. Curse them! I say – I want more to eat than this, Kemp."

"I'll see what there is more to eat downstairs," said Kemp. "Not much, I'm afraid."

After he had done eating – and he made a heavy meal – the Invisible Man demanded a cigar. He bit the end savagely before Kemp could find a knife, and cursed when the outer leaf loosened. It was strange to see him smoking; his mouth and throat, pharynx and nares,* became visible as a sort of whirling smoke cast.

"This blessed gift of smoking!" he said, and puffed vigorously. "I'm lucky to have fallen upon you, Kemp. You must help me. Fancy tumbling on you just now! I'm in a devilish scrape. I've been mad, I think. The things I have been through! But we will do things yet. Let me tell you…"

He helped himself to more whisky and soda. Kemp got up, looked about him and fetched himself a glass from his spare room. "It's wild – but I suppose I may drink."

"You haven't changed much, Kemp, these dozen years. You fair men don't. Cool and methodical – after the first collapse. I must tell you. We will work together!"

"But how was it all done?" said Kemp. "And how did you get like this?"

"For God's sake, let me smoke in peace for a little while! And then I will begin to tell you."

CHAPTER 17

But the story was not told that night. The Invisible Man's wrist was growing painful, he was feverish, exhausted, and his mind came round to brood upon his chase down the hill and the struggle about the inn. He spoke in fragments of Marvel, he smoked faster, his voice grew angry. Kemp tried to gather what he could.

"He was afraid of me, I could see he was afraid of me," said the Invisible Man many times over. "He meant to give me the slip – he was always casting about! What a fool I was!

"The cur!

"I should have killed him—"

"Where did you get the money?" asked Kemp abruptly.

The Invisible Man was silent for a space. "I can't tell you tonight," he said.

He groaned suddenly and leant forward, supporting his invisible head on invisible hands. "Kemp," he said, "I've had no sleep for near three days – except a couple of dozes of an hour or so. I must sleep soon."

"Well, have my room – have this room."

"But how can I sleep? If I sleep – he will get away. Ugh! What does it matter?"

"What's the shot wound?" asked Kemp abruptly.

"Nothing – scratch and blood. Oh, God! How I want sleep!"

"Why not?"

The Invisible Man appeared to be regarding Kemp. "Because I've a particular objection to being caught by my fellow men," he said slowly.

Kemp started.

"Fool that I am!" said the Invisible Man, striking the table smartly. "I've put the idea into your head."

18

The Invisible Man Sleeps

EXHAUSTED AND WOUNDED as the Invisible Man was, he refused to accept Kemp's word that his freedom should be respected. He examined the two windows of the bedroom, drew up the blinds and opened the sashes, to confirm Kemp's statement that a retreat by them would be possible. Outside the night was very quiet and still, and the new moon was setting over the down. Then he examined the keys of the bedroom and the two dressing-room doors, to satisfy himself that these also could be made an assurance of freedom. Finally he expressed himself satisfied. He stood on the hearthrug and Kemp heard the sound of a yawn.

"I'm sorry," said the Invisible Man, "if I cannot tell you all that I have done tonight. But I am worn out. It's grotesque, no doubt. It's horrible! But believe me, Kemp, it is quite a possible thing. I have made a discovery. I meant to keep it to myself. I can't. I must have a partner. And you – we can do such things – but tomorrow. Now, Kemp, I feel as though I must sleep or perish."

Kemp stood in the middle of the room staring at the headless garment. "I suppose I must leave you," he said. "It's – incredible. Three things happening like this, overturning all my preconceptions, would make me insane. But it's real! Is there anything more that I can get you?"

"Only bid me goodnight," said Griffin.

"Goodnight," said Kemp, and shook an invisible hand. He walked sideways to the door. Suddenly the dressing gown walked quickly towards him. "Understand me!" said the dressing gown. "No attempts to hamper me or capture me! Or..."

Kemp's face changed a little. "I thought I gave you my word," he said.

Kemp closed the door softly behind him, and the key was turned upon him forthwith. Then, as he stood with an expression of passive amazement on his face, the rapid feet came to the door of the dressing room and that too was locked. Kemp slapped his brow with his hand. "Am I dreaming? Has the world gone mad – or have I?"

He laughed, and put his hand to the locked door.

"Barred out of my own bedroom, by a flagrant absurdity!" he said.

He walked to the head of the staircase, turned and stared at the locked doors. "It's fact," he said. He put his fingers to his slightly bruised neck. "Undeniable fact!

"But..."

He shook his head hopelessly, turned, and went downstairs. He lit the dining-room lamp, got out a cigar and began pacing the room, ejaculating. Now and then he would argue with himself.

"Invisible!" he said.

"Is there such a thing as an invisible animal? In the sea, yes. Thousands! Millions! All the larvae, all the little nauplii and tornarias,* all the microscopic things, the jellyfish. In the sea there are more things invisible than visible! I never thought of that before. And in the ponds too! All those little pond-life things – specks of colourless translucent jelly! But in air? No!

"It can't be.

"But after all – why not?

"If a man were made of glass he would still be visible."

His meditation became profound. The bulk of three cigars had passed into the invisible or diffused as a white ash over the carpet before he spoke again. Then it was merely an exclamation. He turned aside, walked out of the room and went into his little consulting room and lit the gas there. It was a little room, because Dr Kemp did not live by practice, and in it were the day's newspapers. The morning's paper lay carelessly opened and thrown aside. He caught it up, turned it over and read the account of a "Strange Story from Iping" that the mariner at Port Stowe had spelt over so painfully to Mr Marvel. Kemp read it swiftly.

"Wrapped up!" said Kemp. "Disguised! Hiding it! 'No one seems to have been aware of his misfortune.' What the devil *is* his game?"

He dropped the paper, and his eye went seeking. "Ah!" he said, and caught up the *St James's Gazette*, lying folded up as it arrived. "Now we shall get at the truth," said Dr Kemp. He rent the paper open; a couple of columns confronted him. "An Entire Village in Sussex goes Mad" was the heading.

"Good Heavens!" said Kemp, reading eagerly an incredulous account of the events in Iping the previous afternoon that have already been described. Over the leaf the report in the morning paper had been reprinted.

He reread it. "Ran through the streets striking right and left. Jaffers insensible. Mr Huxter in great pain – still unable to describe what he saw. Painful humiliation – vicar. Woman ill with terror! Windows smashed. This extraordinary story probably a fabrication. Too good not to print – *cum grano!*"*

He dropped the paper and stared blankly in front of him. "Probably a fabrication!"

He caught up the paper again, and reread the whole business. "But when does the tramp come in? Why the deuce was he chasing a tramp?"

He sat down abruptly on the surgical couch. "He's not only invisible," he said, "but he's mad! Homicidal!"

When dawn came to mingle its pallor with the lamplight and cigar smoke of the dining room, Kemp was still pacing up and down, trying to grasp the incredible.

He was altogether too excited to sleep. His servants, descending sleepily, discovered him, and were inclined to think that over-study had worked this ill on him. He gave them extraordinary but quite explicit instructions to lay breakfast for two in the belvedere study – and then to confine themselves to the basement and ground floor. Then he continued to pace the dining room until the morning's paper came. That had much to say and little to tell, beyond the confirmation of the evening before and a very baldly written account of another remarkable tale from Port Burdock. This gave Kemp the essence of the happenings at the Jolly Cricketers, and the name of Marvel. "He has made me keep with him twenty-four hours," Marvel testified. Certain minor facts were added to the Iping story, notably the cutting of the village telegraph wire. But there was nothing to throw light on the connection between the Invisible Man and the tramp; for Mr Marvel had supplied no information about the three books or the money with which he was lined. The incredulous tone had vanished and a shoal of reporters and enquirers were already at work elaborating the matter.

Kemp read every scrap of the report, and sent his housemaid out to get every one of the morning papers she could. These also he devoured.

"He is invisible!" he said. "And it reads like rage growing to mania! The things he may do! The things he may do! And he's upstairs free as the air. What on earth ought I to do?

"For instance, would it be a breach of faith if?… No."

He went to a little untidy desk in the corner and began a note. He tore this up half written, and wrote another. He read it over and considered it. Then he took an envelope and addressed it to "Colonel Adye, Port Burdock".

The Invisible Man awoke even as Kemp was doing this. He awoke in an evil temper, and Kemp, alert for every sound, heard his pattering feet rush suddenly across the bedroom overhead. Then a chair was flung over and the wash-hand-stand tumbler smashed. Kemp hurried upstairs and rapped eagerly.

19

Certain First Principles

"WHAT'S THE MATTER?" asked Kemp when the Invisible Man admitted him.

"Nothing," was the answer.

"But, confound it! The smash?"

"Fit of temper," said the Invisible Man. "Forgot this arm – and it's sore."

"You're rather liable to that sort of thing."

"I am."

Kemp walked across the room and picked up the fragments of broken glass. "All the facts are out about you," said Kemp, standing up with the glass in his hand. "All that happened in Iping, and down the hill. The world has become aware of its invisible citizen. But no one knows you are here."

The Invisible Man swore.

"The secret's out. I gather it was a secret. I don't know what your plans are, but of course I'm anxious to help you."

The Invisible Man sat down on the bed.

"There's breakfast upstairs," said Kemp, speaking as easily as possible, and he was delighted to find his strange guest rose willingly. Kemp led the way up the narrow staircase to the belvedere.

"Before we can do anything else," said Kemp, "I must understand a little more about this invisibility of yours." He had sat down, after one nervous glance out of the window, with the air of a man who has talking to do. His doubts of the sanity of the entire business flashed and vanished again as he looked across to where Griffin sat at the breakfast table – a headless, handless dressing gown, wiping unseen lips on a miraculously held serviette.

"It's simple enough – and credible enough," said Griffin, putting the serviette aside.

"No doubt, to you, but…" Kemp laughed.

"Well, yes: to me it seemed wonderful at first, no doubt. But now, great God! But we will do great things yet! I came on the stuff first at Chesilstowe."

"Chesilstowe?"

"I went there after I left London. You know I dropped medicine and took up physics? No? Well, I did. Light – fascinated me."

"Ah!"

"Optical density! The whole subject is a network of riddles – a network with solutions glimmering elusively through. And being but two-and-twenty and full of enthusiasm, I said, 'I will devote my life to this. This is worthwhile.' You know what fools we are at two-and-twenty?"

"Fools then or fools now," said Kemp.

"As though knowing could be any satisfaction to a man!

"But I went to work – like a nigger. And I had hardly worked and thought about the matter six months before light came through one of the meshes suddenly – blindingly! I found a general principle of pigments and refraction, a formula, a geometrical expression involving four dimensions. Fools, common men, even common mathematicians, do not know anything of what some general expression may mean to the student of molecular physics. In the books – the books that tramp has hidden – there are marvels, miracles! But this was not a method, it was an idea that might lead to a method by which it would be possible, without changing any other property of matter – except, in some instances, colours – to lower the refractive index of a substance, solid or liquid, to that of air – so far as all practical purposes are concerned."

"Phew!" said Kemp. "That's odd! But still I don't see quite… I can understand that thereby you could spoil a valuable stone, but personal invisibility is a far cry."

"Precisely," said Griffin. "But consider: visibility depends on the action of the visible bodies on light. Either a body absorbs light, or it reflects or refracts it, or does all these things. If it neither reflects nor refracts nor absorbs light, it cannot of itself be visible. You see an opaque red box, for instance, because the colour absorbs some of the light and reflects the rest, all the red part of the light, to you. If it did not absorb any particular part of the light, but reflected it all, then it would be a shining white box. Silver! A diamond box would neither absorb much of the light nor reflect much from the general surface, but just here and there where the surfaces were favourable the light would be reflected and refracted, so that you would get a brilliant appearance of flashing reflections and translucencies – a sort of skeleton of light. A glass box would not be so brilliant, not so clearly visible, as a diamond box, because there would be less refraction and reflection. See that? From certain points of view you would see quite clearly through it. Some kinds of glass would be more visible than others, a box of flint glass would be brighter than a box of ordinary window glass. A box of very thin common glass would be hard to see in a bad light, because it would absorb hardly any light and refract and reflect very little. And if you put a sheet of common white glass in water, still more if you put it in some denser liquid than water, it would vanish almost altogether, because light passing from water to glass is only slightly refracted or reflected or indeed affected in any way. It is almost as invisible as a jet of coal gas or hydrogen is in air. And for precisely the same reason!"

"Yes," said Kemp, "that is pretty plain sailing."

"And here is another fact you will know to be true. If a sheet of glass is smashed, Kemp, and beaten into a powder, it becomes much more visible while it is in the air; it becomes at last an opaque white powder. This is because the powdering multiplies the surfaces of the glass at which refraction and reflection occur. In the sheet of glass there are only two surfaces; in the powder the light is reflected or refracted by each grain it passes through, and very little gets right through the powder. But if the white powdered glass is put into water, it forthwith vanishes. The powdered glass and water have much the same refractive index: that is, the light undergoes very little refraction or reflection in passing from one to the other.

"You make the glass invisible by putting it into a liquid of nearly the same refractive index; a transparent thing becomes invisible if it is put in any medium of almost the same refractive index. And if you will consider only a second, you will see also that the powder of glass might be made to vanish in air, if its refractive index could be made the same as that of air; for then there would be no refraction or reflection as the light passed from glass to air."

"Yes, yes," said Kemp. "But a man's not powdered glass!"

"No," said Griffin. "He's more transparent!"

"Nonsense!"

"That from a doctor! How one forgets! Have you already forgotten your physics, in ten years? Just think of all the things that are transparent and seem not to be so. Paper, for instance, is made up of transparent fibres, and it is white and opaque only for the same reason that a powder of glass is white and opaque. Oil white paper, fill up the interstices between the particles with oil so that there is no longer refraction or reflection except at the surfaces, and it becomes as transparent as glass. And not only paper, but cotton fibre, linen fibre, wool fibre, woody fibre, and *bone*, Kemp, *flesh*, Kemp, *hair*, Kemp, *nails* and *nerves*, Kemp, in fact the whole fabric of a man except the red of his blood and the black pigment of hair, are all made up of transparent, colourless tissue. So little suffices to make us visible one to the other. For the most part the fibres of a living creature are no more opaque than water."

"Great Heavens!" cried Kemp. "Of course, of course! I was thinking only last night of the sea larvae and all jellyfish!"

"*Now* you have me! And all that I knew and had in mind a year after I left London – six years ago. But I kept it to myself. I had to do my work under frightful disadvantages. Oliver, my professor, was a scientific bounder, a journalist by instinct, a thief of ideas – he was always prying! And you know the knavish system of the scientific world. I simply would not publish, and let him share my credit. I went on working, I got nearer and nearer making my formula into an experiment, a reality. I told no living soul, because I meant to flash my work upon the world with crushing effect – to become famous at a blow. I took up the question of pigments to fill up certain gaps. And suddenly, not by design but by accident, I made a discovery in physiology."

"Yes?"

"You know the red colouring matter of blood: it can be made white – colourless – and remain with all the functions it has now!"

Kemp gave a cry of incredulous amazement.

The Invisible Man rose and began pacing the little study. "You may well exclaim. I remember that night. It was late at night – in the daytime one was bothered with the gaping, silly students – and I worked then sometimes till dawn. It came suddenly, splendid and complete into my mind. I was alone; the laboratory was still, with the tall lights burning brightly and silently. In all my great moments I have been alone. 'One could make an animal – a tissue – transparent! One could make it invisible! All except the pigments. I could be invisible!' I said, suddenly realizing what it meant to be an albino with such knowledge. It was overwhelming. I left the filtering I was doing, and went and stared out of the great window at the stars. 'I could be invisible!' I repeated.

"To do such a thing would be to transcend magic. And I beheld, unclouded by doubt, a magnificent vision of all that invisibility might mean to a man – the mystery, the power, the freedom. Drawbacks I saw none. You have only to think! And I, a shabby, poverty-struck, hemmed-in demonstrator, teaching fools in a provincial college, might suddenly become – this. I ask you, Kemp, if *you* – anyone, I tell you, would have flung himself upon that research. And I worked three years, and every mountain of difficulty I toiled over showed another from its summit. The infinite details! And the exasperation – a professor, a provincial professor, always prying. 'When are you going to publish this work of yours?' was his everlasting question. And the students, the cramped means! Three years I had of it…

"And after three years of secrecy and exasperation, I found that to complete it was impossible – impossible."

"How?" asked Kemp.

"Money," said the Invisible Man, and went again to stare out of the window.

He turned round abruptly. "I robbed the old man – robbed my father.

"The money was not his, and he shot himself."

20

At the House in Great Portland Street

F OR A MOMENT KEMP SAT in silence, staring at the back of the headless figure at the window. Then he started, struck by a thought, rose, took the Invisible Man's arm and turned him away from the outlook.

"You are tired," he said, "and while I sit, you walk about. Have my chair."

He placed himself between Griffin and the nearest window.

For a space Griffin sat silent, and then he resumed abruptly:

"I had left the Chesilstowe College already," he said, "when that happened. It was last December. I had taken a room in London, a large unfurnished room in a big ill-managed lodging house in a slum near Great Portland Street. The room was soon full of the appliances I had bought with his money; the work was going on steadily, successfully, drawing near an end. I was like a man emerging from a thicket, and suddenly coming on some unmeaning tragedy. I went to bury my father. My mind was still on this research, and I did not lift a finger to save his character. I remember the funeral, the cheap hearse, the scant ceremony, the windy frostbitten hillside and the old college friend of his who read the service over him – a shabby, black, bent old man with a snivelling cold.

"I remember walking back to the empty home, through the place that had once been a village and was now patched and tinkered by the jerry builders into the ugly likeness of a town. Every way the roads ran out at last into the desecrated fields and ended in rubble heaps and rank wet weeds. I remember myself as a gaunt black figure, going along the slippery, shiny sidewalk, and the strange sense of detachment I felt from the squalid respectability, the sordid commercialism of the place.

"I did not feel a bit sorry for my father. He seemed to me to be the victim of his own foolish sentimentality. The current cant required my attendance at his funeral, but it was really not my affair.

"But going along the High Street, my old life came back to me for a space, for I met the girl I had known ten years since. Our eyes met.

"Something moved me to turn back and talk to her. She was a very ordinary person.

"It was all like a dream, that visit to the old place. I did not feel then that I was lonely, that I had come out from the world into a desolation. I appreciated my loss of sympathy, but I put it down to the general inanity of life. Re-entering my room seemed like the recovery of reality. There were the things I knew and loved. There stood the apparatus, the experiments arranged and waiting. And now there was scarcely a difficulty left, beyond the planning of details.

"I will tell you, Kemp, sooner or later, all the complicated processes. We need not go into that now. For the most part, saving certain gaps I chose to remember, they are written in cipher in those books that tramp has hidden. We must hunt him down. We must get those books again. But the essential phase was to place the transparent object whose refractive index was to be lowered between two radiating centres of a sort of ethereal vibration, of which I will tell you more fully later. No, not these Röntgen vibrations* – I don't know that these others of mine have been described. Yet they are obvious enough. I needed two little dynamos, and these I worked with a cheap gas engine. My first experiment was with a bit of white wool fabric. It was the strangest thing in the world to see it in the flicker of the flashes soft and white, and then to watch it fade like a wreath of smoke and vanish.

"I could scarcely believe I had done it. I put my hand into the emptiness, and there was the thing as solid as ever. I felt it awkwardly, and threw it on the floor. I had a little trouble finding it again.

"And then came a curious experience. I heard a miaow behind me and, turning, saw a lean white cat, very dirty, on the cistern cover outside the window. A thought came into my head. 'Everything ready for you,' I said, and went to the window, opened it and called softly. She came in, purring – the poor beast was starving – and I gave her some milk. All my food was in a cupboard in the corner of the room. After that she went smelling round the room – evidently with the idea of making herself at home. The invisible rag upset her a bit; you should have seen her spit at it! But I made her comfortable on the pillow of my truckle bed. And I gave her butter to get her to wash."

"And you processed her?"

"I processed her. But giving drugs to a cat is no joke, Kemp! And the process failed."

"Failed!"

"In two particulars. These were the claws and the pigment stuff – what is it? – at the back of the eye in a cat. You know?"

"*Tapetum.*"*

"Yes, the *tapetum*. It didn't go. After I'd given the stuff to bleach the blood and done certain other things to her, I gave the beast opium, and put her and the pillow she was sleeping on on the apparatus. And after all the rest had faded and vanished, there remained two little ghosts of her eyes."

"Odd!"

"I can't explain it. She was bandaged and clamped, of course – so I had her safe; but she woke while she was still misty, and miaowed dismally, and someone came knocking. It was an old woman from downstairs, who suspected me of vivisecting – a drink-sodden old creature, with only a white cat to care for in all the world. I whipped out some chloroform, and applied it, and answered the door. 'Did I hear a cat?' she asked. 'My cat?' 'Not here,' said I, very politely. She was a little doubtful and tried to peer past me into the room; strange enough to her no doubt – bare walls, uncurtained windows, truckle bed, with the gas engine vibrating, and the seethe of the radiant points, and that faint ghastly stinging of chloroform in the air. She had to be satisfied at last and went away again."

"How long did it take?" asked Kemp.

"Three or four hours – the cat. The bones and sinews and the fat were the last to go, and the tips of the coloured hairs. And, as I say, the back part of the eye – tough iridescent stuff it is – wouldn't go at all.

"It was night outside long before the business was over, and nothing was to be seen but the dim eyes and the claws. I stopped the gas engine, felt for and stroked the beast, which was still insensible, released its fastenings, and then, being tired, left it sleeping on the invisible pillow and went to bed. I found it hard to sleep. I lay awake thinking weak aimless stuff, going over the experiment over and over again, or dreaming feverishly of things growing misty and vanishing about me, until everything, the ground I stood on, vanished, and so I came to that sickly falling nightmare one gets. About two, the cat began miaowing about the room. I tried to hush it by talking to it, and then I decided to turn it out. I remember the shock I had when striking a light – there were just the round eyes shining green – and nothing round them. I would have given it milk, but I hadn't any. It wouldn't be quiet, it just sat down and miaowed at the door. I tried to catch it, with an idea of putting it out of the window, but it wouldn't be caught: it vanished. Then it began miaowing in different parts of the room. At last I opened the window and made a bustle. I suppose it went out at last. I never saw any more of it.

"Then – Heaven knows why – I fell thinking of my father's funeral again, and the dismal windy hillside, until the day had come. I found sleeping was hopeless and, locking my door after me, wandered out into the morning streets."

"You don't mean to say there's an invisible cat at large!" said Kemp.

"If it hasn't been killed," said the Invisible Man. "Why not?"

"Why not?" said Kemp. "I didn't mean to interrupt."

"It's very probably been killed," said the Invisible Man. "It was alive four days after, I know, and down a grating in Great Titchfield Street – because I saw a crowd round the place, trying to see whence the miaowing came."

He was silent for the best part of a minute. Then he resumed abruptly:

"I remember that morning before the change very vividly. I must have gone up Great Portland Street. I remember the barracks in Albany Street, and the horse soldiers coming out, and at last I found myself sitting in the sunshine and feeling very ill and strange, on the summit of Primrose Hill. It was a sunny day in January – one of those sunny, frosty days that came before the snow this year. My weary brain tried to formulate the position, to plot out a plan of action.

"I was surprised to find, now that my prize was within my grasp, how inconclusive its attainment seemed. As a matter of fact I was worked out: the intense stress of nearly four years' continuous work left me incapable of any strength of feeling. I was apathetic, and I tried in vain to recover the enthusiasm of my first enquiries, the passion of discovery that had enabled me to compass even the downfall of my father's grey hairs. Nothing seemed to matter. I saw pretty clearly this was a transient mood, due to overwork and want of sleep, and that either by drugs or rest it would be possible to recover my energies.

"All I could think clearly was that the thing had to be carried through – the fixed idea still ruled me. And soon, for the money I had was almost exhausted. I looked about me at the hillside, with children playing and girls watching them, and tried to think of all the fantastic advantages an invisible man would have in the world. After a time I crawled home, took some food and a strong dose of strychnine, and went to sleep in my clothes on my unmade bed. Strychnine is a grand tonic, Kemp, to take the flabbiness out of a man."

"It's the devil," said Kemp. "It's the Palaeolithic in a bottle."*

"I awoke vastly invigorated and rather irritable. You know?"

"I know the stuff."

"And there was someone rapping at the door. It was my landlord with threats and enquiries, an old Polish Jew in a long grey coat and greasy slippers. I had been tormenting a cat in the night, he was sure – the old woman's tongue had been busy. He insisted on knowing all about it. The laws of this country against vivisection were very severe – he might be liable. I denied the cat. Then the vibration of the little gas engine could be felt all over the house, he said. That was true, certainly. He edged round me into the room, peering about over his German silver* spectacles, and a sudden dread came into my mind that he might carry away something of my secret. I tried to keep between him and the concentrating apparatus I had arranged, and that only made him more curious. What was I doing? Why was I always alone and secretive? Was it legal? Was it dangerous? I paid nothing but the usual rent. His had always been a most respectable house – in a disreputable neighbourhood. Suddenly my temper gave way. I told him to get out. He began to protest, to jabber of his right of entry. In a moment I had him by the collar; something ripped, and he went spinning out into his own passage. I slammed and locked the door and sat down quivering.

"He made a fuss outside, which I disregarded, and after a time he went away.

"But this brought matters to a crisis. I did not know what he would do, nor even what he had power to do. To move to fresh apartments would have meant delay; all together I had barely twenty pounds left in the world – for the most part in a bank – and I could not afford that. Vanish! It was irresistible. Then there would be an inquiry, the sacking of my room...

"At the thought of the possibility of my work being exposed or interrupted at its very climax, I became angry and active. I hurried out with my three books of notes, my chequebook – the tramp has them now – and directed them from the nearest post office to a house of call for letters and parcels in Great Portland Street. I tried to go out noiselessly. Coming in, I found my landlord going quietly upstairs; he had heard the door close, I suppose. You would have laughed to see him jump aside on the landing as I came tearing after him. He glared at me as I went by him, and I made the house quiver with the slamming of my door. I heard him come shuffling up to my floor, hesitate and go down. I set to work upon my preparations forthwith.

"It was all done that evening and night. While I was still sitting under the sickly, drowsy influence of the drugs that decolourize blood, there came a repeated knocking at the door. It ceased, footsteps went away and returned, and the knocking was resumed. There was an attempt to push something under the door – a blue paper. Then in a fit of irritation I rose and went and flung the door wide open. 'Now then?' said I.

"It was my landlord, with a notice of ejectment or something. He held it out to me, saw something odd about my hands, I expect, and lifted his eyes to my face.

"For a moment he gaped. Then he gave a sort of inarticulate cry, dropped candle and writ together and went blundering down the dark passage to the stairs. I shut the door, locked it and went to the looking glass. Then I understood his terror. My face was white – like white stone.

"But it was all horrible. I had not expected the suffering. A night of racking anguish, sickness and fainting. I set my teeth, though my skin was presently afire, all my body afire; but I lay there like grim death. I understood now how it was the cat had howled until I chloroformed it. Lucky it was I lived alone and untended in my room. There were times when I sobbed and groaned and talked. But I stuck to it. I became insensible and woke languid in the darkness.

"The pain had passed. I thought I was killing myself and I did not care. I shall never forget that dawn, and the strange horror of seeing that my hands had become as clouded glass, and watching them grow clearer and thinner as the day went by, until at last I could see the sickly disorder of my room through them, though I closed my transparent eyelids. My limbs became glassy, the bones and arteries faded, vanished, and the little white nerves went last. I ground my teeth and stayed there to the end. At last only the dead tips of the fingernails remained, pallid and white, and the brown stain of some acid upon my fingers.

"I struggled up. At first I was as incapable as a swathed infant – stepping with limbs I could not see. I was weak and very hungry. I went and stared at nothing in my shaving glass, at nothing save where an attenuated pigment still remained behind the retina of my eyes, fainter than mist. I had to hang on to the table and press my forehead to the glass.

"It was only by a frantic effort of will that I dragged myself back to the apparatus and completed the process.

"I slept during the forenoon, pulling the sheet over my eyes to shut out the light, and about midday I was awakened again by a knocking. My strength had returned. I sat up and listened and heard a whispering. I sprang to my feet and as noiselessly as possible began to detach the connections of my apparatus, and to distribute it about the room, so as to destroy the suggestions of its arrangement. Presently the knocking was renewed and voices called, first my landlord's and then two others. To gain time I answered them. The invisible rag and pillow came to hand and I opened the window and pitched them out onto the cistern cover. As the window opened, a heavy crash came at the door. Someone had charged it with the idea of smashing the lock. But the stout bolts I had screwed up some days before stopped him. That startled me, made me angry. I began to tremble and do things hurriedly.

"I tossed together some loose paper, straw, packing paper and so forth, in the middle of the room, and turned on the gas. Heavy blows began to rain upon the door. I could not find the matches. I beat my hands on the wall with rage. I turned down the gas again, stepped out of the window on the cistern cover, very softly lowered the sash and sat down, secure and invisible, but quivering with anger, to watch events. They split a panel, I saw, and in another moment they had broken away the staples of the bolts and stood in the open doorway. It was the landlord and his two stepsons, sturdy young men of three- or four-and-twenty. Behind them fluttered the old hag of a woman from downstairs.

"You may imagine their astonishment on finding the room empty. One of the younger men rushed to the window at once, flung it up and stared out. His staring eyes and thick-lipped, bearded face came a foot from my face. I was half minded to hit his silly countenance, but I arrested my doubled fist. He stared right through me. So did the others as they joined him. The old man went and peered under the bed, and then they all made a rush for the cupboard. They had to argue about it at length in Yiddish and cockney English. They concluded I had not answered them, that their imagination had deceived them. A feeling of extraordinary elation took the place of my anger as I sat outside the window and watched these four people – for the old lady came in, glancing suspiciously about her like a cat, trying to understand the riddle of my behaviour.

"The old man, so far as I could understand his patois, agreed with the old lady that I was a vivisectionist. The sons protested in garbled English that I was an electrician, and appealed to the dynamos and radiators. They were all nervous against my arrival, although I found subsequently that they had bolted the front door. The old lady peered into the cupboard and under the bed, and one of the young men pushed up the register and stared up the chimney. One of my fellow lodgers, a costermonger who shared the opposite room with a butcher, appeared on the landing, and he was called in and told incoherent things.

"It occurred to me that the radiators, if they fell into the hands of some acute well-educated person, would give me away too much, and, watching my opportunity, I came into the room and tilted one of the little dynamos off its fellow on which it was standing, and smashed both apparatus. Then, while they were trying to explain the smash, I dodged out of the room and went softly downstairs.

"I went into one of the sitting rooms and waited until they came down, still speculating and argumentative, all a little disappointed at finding no 'horrors', and all a little puzzled how they stood with regard to me. Then I slipped up again with a box of matches, fired my heap of paper and rubbish, put the chairs and bedding thereby, led the gas to the affair, by means of an India-rubber tube, and, waving a farewell to the room, left it for the last time."

"You fired the house!" exclaimed Kemp.

"Fired the house. It was the only way to cover my trail – and no doubt it was insured. I slipped the bolts of the front door quietly and went out into the street. I was invisible, and I was only just beginning to realize the extraordinary advantage my invisibility gave me. My head was already teeming with plans of all the wild and wonderful things I had now impunity to do."

21

In Oxford Street

"IN GOING DOWNSTAIRS the first time I found an unexpected difficulty because I could not see my feet; indeed I stumbled twice, and there was an unaccustomed clumsiness in gripping the bolt. By not looking down, however, I managed to walk on the level passably well.

"My mood, I say, was one of exaltation. I felt as a seeing man might do, with padded feet and noiseless clothes, in a city of the blind. I experienced a wild impulse to jest, to startle people, to clap men on the back, fling people's hats astray and generally revel in my extraordinary advantage.

"But hardly had I emerged upon Great Portland Street, however (my lodging was close to the big draper's shop there), when I heard a clashing concussion and was hit violently behind, and turning saw a man carrying a basket of soda-water syphons and looking in amazement at his burden. Although the blow had really hurt me, I found something so irresistible in his astonishment that I laughed aloud. 'The devil's in the basket,' I said, and suddenly twisted it out of his hand. He let go incontinently, and I swung the whole weight into the air.

"But a fool of a cabman, standing outside a public house, made a sudden rush for this, and his extending fingers took me with excruciating violence under the ear. I let the whole down with a smash on the cabman, and then, with shouts and the clatter of feet about me, people coming out of shops, vehicles pulling up, I realized what I had done for myself and, cursing my folly, backed against a shop window and prepared to dodge out of the confusion. In a moment I should be wedged into a crowd and inevitably discovered. I pushed by a butcher boy, who luckily did not turn to see the nothingness that shoved him aside, and dodged behind the cabman's four-wheeler. I do not know how they settled the business. I hurried straight across the road, which was happily clear, and hardly heeding which way I went, in the fright of detection the incident had given me, plunged into the afternoon throng of Oxford Street.

"I tried to get into the stream of people, but they were too thick for me, and in a moment my heels were being trodden upon. I took to the gutter, the roughness of which I found painful to my feet, and forthwith the shaft of a crawling hansom dug me forcibly under the shoulder blade, reminding me that I was already bruised severely. I staggered out of the way of the cab, avoided a perambulator by a convulsive movement and found myself behind the hansom.* A happy thought saved me, and as this drove slowly along I followed in its immediate wake, trembling and astonished at the turn of my adventure. And not only trembling, but shivering. It was a bright day in January and I was stark naked and the thin slime of mud that covered the road was freezing. Foolish as it seems to me now, I had not reckoned that, transparent or not, I was still amenable to the weather and all its consequences.

"Then suddenly a bright idea came into my head. I ran round and got into the cab. And so, shivering, scared and sniffing with the first intimations of a cold, and with the bruises in the small of my back growing upon my attention, I drove slowly along Oxford Street and past Tottenham Court Road. My mood was as different from that in which I had sallied forth ten minutes ago as it is possible to imagine. *This* invisibility indeed! The one thought that possessed me was how to get out of the scrape I was in.

"We crawled past Mudie's,* and there a tall woman with five or six yellow-labelled books hailed my cab, and I sprang out just in time to escape her, shaving a railway van narrowly in my flight. I made off up the roadway to Bloomsbury Square, intending to strike north past the Museum* and so get into the quiet district. I was now cruelly chilled, and the strangeness of my situation so unnerved me that I whimpered as I ran. At the westward corner of the square a little white dog ran out of the Pharmaceutical Society's offices and incontinently made for me, nose down.

"I had never realized it before, but the nose is to the mind of a dog what the eye is to the mind of a seeing man. Dogs perceive the scent of a man moving as men perceive his vision. This brute began barking and leaping, showing, as it seemed to me, only too plainly that he was aware of me. I crossed Great Russell Street, glancing over my shoulder as I did so, and went some way along Montague Street before I realized what I was running towards.

"Then I became aware of a blare of music, and looking along the street saw a number of people advancing out of Russell Square, red shirts and the banner of the Salvation Army to the fore. Such a crowd, chanting in the roadway and scoffing on the pavement, I could not hope to penetrate and, dreading to go back and farther from home again and deciding on the spur of the moment, I ran up the white steps of a house facing the Museum railings, and stood there until the crowd should have passed. Happily the dog stopped at the noise of the band too, hesitated and turned tail, running back to Bloomsbury Square again.

"On came the band, bawling with unconscious irony some hymn about 'When Shall We See His Face?'* and it seemed an interminable time to me before the tide of the crowd washed along the pavement by me. Thud, thud, thud, came the drum with a vibrating resonance, and for the moment I did not notice two urchins stopping at the railings by me. 'See 'em,' said one. 'See what?' said the other. 'Why – them footmarks – *bare*. Like what you makes in mud.'

"I looked down and saw the youngsters had stopped and were gaping at the muddy footmarks I had left behind me up the newly whitened steps. The passing people elbowed and jostled them, but their confounded intelligence was arrested. 'Thud, thud, thud, When, thud, shall we see, thud, his face, thud, thud.' 'There's a barefoot man gone up them steps, or I don't know nothing,' said one. 'And he ain't never come down again. And his foot was a-bleeding.'

"The thick of the crowd had already passed. 'Looky there, Ted,' quoth the younger of the detectives, with the sharpness of surprise in his voice, and pointed straight to my feet. I looked down and saw at once the dim suggestion of their outline sketched in splashes of mud. For a moment I was paralysed.

"'Why, that's rum,' said the elder. 'Dashed rum! It's just like the ghost of a foot, ain't it?' He hesitated and advanced with outstretched hand. A man pulled up short to see what he was catching, and then a girl. In another moment he would have touched me. Then I saw what to do. I made a step, the boy started back with an exclamation, and with a rapid movement I swung myself over into the portico of the next house. But the smaller boy was sharp-eyed enough to follow the movement, and before I was well down the steps and upon the pavement, he had recovered from his momentary astonishment and was shouting out that the feet had gone over the wall.

"They rushed round and saw my new footmarks flash into being on the lower step and upon the pavement. 'What's up?' asked someone. 'Feet! Look! Feet running!' Everybody in the road, except my three pursuers, was pouring along after the Salvation Army, and this not only impeded me but them. There was an eddy of surprise and interrogation. At the cost of bowling over one young fellow I got through, and in another moment I was rushing headlong round the circuit of Russell Square, with six or seven astonished people following my foot-marks. There was no time for explanation, or else the whole host would have been after me.

"Twice I doubled round corners, thrice I crossed the road and came back on my tracks, and then, as my feet grew hot and dry, the damp impressions began to fade. At last I had a breathing space and rubbed my feet clean with my hands, and so got away altogether. The last I saw of the chase was a little group of a dozen people perhaps, studying with infinite perplexity a slowly drying footprint that had resulted from a puddle in Tavistock Square – a footprint as isolated and incomprehensible to them as Crusoe's solitary discovery.*

"This running warmed me to a certain extent, and I went on with a better courage through the maze of less frequented roads that runs thereabout. My back had now become very stiff and sore, my tonsils were painful from the cabman's fingers and the skin of my neck had been scratched by his nails; my feet hurt exceedingly and I was lame from a little cut on one foot. I saw in time a blind man approaching me, and fled limping, for I feared his subtle intuitions. Once or twice accidental collisions occurred and I left people amazed, with unaccountable curses ringing in their ears. Then came something silent and quiet against my face, and across the square fell a thin veil of slowly falling flakes of snow. I had caught a cold, and do as I would I could not avoid an occasional sneeze. And every dog that came in sight, with its pointing nose and curious sniffing, was a terror to me.

"Then came men and boys running, first one and then others, and shouting as they ran. It was a fire. They ran in the direction of my lodging, and looking back down a street I saw a mass of black smoke streaming up above the roofs and telephone wires. It was my lodging burning: my clothes, my apparatus, all my resources indeed, except my chequebook and the three volumes of memoranda that awaited me in Great Portland Street, were there. Burning! I had burnt my boats – if ever a man did! The place was blazing."

The Invisible Man paused and thought. Kemp glanced nervously out of the window. "Yes?" he said. "Go on."

22

In the Emporium

"SO LAST JANUARY, with the beginnings of a snowstorm in the air about me – and if it settled on me it would betray me! – weary, cold, painful, inexpressibly wretched, and still but half convinced of my invisible quality, I began this new life to which I am committed. I had no refuge, no appliances, no human being in the world in whom I could confide. To have told my secret would have given me away – made a mere show and rarity of me. Nevertheless, I was half minded to accost some passer-by and throw myself upon his mercy. But I knew too clearly the terror and brutal cruelty my advances would evoke. I made no plans in the street. My sole object was to get shelter from the snow, to get myself covered and warm; then I might hope to plan. But even to me, an invisible man, the rows of London houses stood latched, barred and bolted impregnably.

"Only one thing could I see clearly before me: the cold exposure and misery of the snowstorm and the night.

"And then I had a brilliant idea. I turned down one of the roads leading from Gower Street to Tottenham Court Road, and found myself outside Omniums, the big establishment where everything is to be bought – you know the place – meat, grocery, linen, furniture, clothing, oil paintings even – a huge meandering collection of shops rather than a shop. I had thought I should find the doors open, but they were closed, and as I stood in the wide entrance a carriage stopped outside, and a man in uniform – you know the kind of personage with "Omnium" on his cap – flung open the door. I contrived to enter and, walking down the shop – it was a department where they were selling ribbons and gloves and stockings and that kind of thing – came to a more spacious region devoted to picnic baskets and wicker furniture.

"I did not feel safe there, however; people were going to and fro, and I prowled restlessly about until I came upon a huge section in an upper floor containing scores and hundreds of bedsteads, and beyond these I found a resting place at last among a huge pile of folded flock mattresses. The place was already lit up and agreeably warm, and I decided to remain where I was, keeping a cautious eye on the two or three sets of shopmen and customers who were meandering through the place until closing time came. Then I should be able, I thought, to rob the place for food and clothing and, disguised, prowl through it and examine its resources, perhaps sleep on some of the bedding. That seemed an acceptable plan. My idea was to procure clothing to make myself a muffled but acceptable figure, to get money, and then to recover my books and parcels where they awaited me, take a lodging somewhere and elaborate plans for the complete realization of the advantages my invisibility gave me (as I still imagined) over my fellow men.

"Closing time arrived quickly enough; it could not have been more than an hour after I took up my position on the mattresses before I noticed the blinds of the windows being drawn, and customers being marched doorward. And then a number of brisk young men began with remarkable alacrity to tidy up the goods that remained disturbed. I left my lair as the crowds diminished, and prowled cautiously out into the less desolate parts of the shop. I was really surprised to observe how rapidly the young men and women whipped away the goods displayed for sale during the day. All the boxes of goods, the hanging fabrics, the festoons of lace, the boxes of sweets in the grocery section, the displays of this and that, were being whipped down, folded up, slapped into tidy receptacles, and everything that could not be taken down and put away had sheets of some coarse stuff like sacking flung over it. Finally all the chairs were turned up onto the counters, leaving the floor clear. Directly each of these young people had done, he or she made promptly for the door with such an expression of animation as I have rarely observed in a shop assistant before. Then came a lot of youngsters scattering sawdust and carrying pails and brooms. I had to dodge to get out of the way, and as it was, my ankle got stung with the sawdust. For some time, wandering through the swathed and darkened departments, I could hear the brooms at work. And at last, a good hour or more after the shop had been closed, came a noise of locking doors. Silence came upon the place, and I found myself wandering through the vast and intricate shops, galleries and showrooms of the place, alone. It was very still; in one place I remember passing near one of the Tottenham Court Road entrances and listening to the tapping of boot heels of the passers-by.

"My first visit was to the place where I had seen stockings and gloves for sale. It was dark, and I had the devil of a hunt after matches, which I found at last in the drawer of the little cash desk. Then I had to get a candle. I had to tear down wrappings and ransack a number of boxes and drawers, but at last I managed to turn out what I sought: the box label called them lambswool pants and lambswool vests. Then socks, a thick comforter, and then I went to the clothing place and got trousers, a lounge jacket, an overcoat and a slouch hat – a clerical sort of hat with the brim turned down. I began to feel a human being again, and my next thought was food.

"Upstairs was a refreshment department, and there I got cold meat. There was coffee still in the urn, and I lit the gas and warmed it up again, and altogether I did not do badly. Afterwards, prowling through the place in search of blankets – I had to put up at last with a heap of down quilts – I came upon a grocery section with a lot of chocolate and candied fruits, more than was good for me indeed – and some white burgundy. And near that was a toy department, and I had a brilliant idea. I found some artificial noses – dummy noses, you know, and I thought of dark spectacles. But Omniums had no optical department. My nose had been a difficulty indeed – I had thought of paint. But the discovery set my mind running on wigs and masks and the like. Finally I went to sleep in a heap of down quilts, very warm and comfortable.

"My last thoughts before sleeping were the most agreeable I had had since the change. I was in a state of physical serenity, and that was reflected in my mind. I thought that I should be able to slip out unobserved in the morning with my clothes upon me, muffling my face with a white wrapper I had taken, purchase, with the money I had taken, spectacles and so forth, and so complete my disguise. I lapsed into disorderly dreams of all the fantastic things that had happened during the last few days. I saw the ugly little Jew of a landlord vociferating in his rooms; I saw his two sons marvelling, and the wrinkled old woman's gnarled face as she asked for her cat. I experienced again the strange sensation of seeing the cloth disappear, and so I came round to the windy hillside and the sniffing old clergyman mumbling 'Dust to dust, earth to earth',* and my father's open grave.

"'You also,' said a voice, and suddenly I was being forced towards the grave. I struggled, shouted, appealed to the mourners, but they continued stonily following the service; the old clergyman, too, never faltered droning and sniffing through the ritual. I realized I was invisible and inaudible, that overwhelming forces had their grip on me. I struggled in vain: I was forced over the brink, the coffin rang hollow as I fell upon it and the gravel came flying after me in spadefuls. Nobody heeded me, nobody was aware of me. I made convulsive struggles and awoke.

"The pale London dawn had come, the place was full of a chilly grey light that filtered round the edges of the window blinds. I sat up, and for a time I could not think where this ample apartment – with its counters, its piles of rolled stuff, its heap of quilts and cushions, its iron pillars – might be. Then, as recollection came back to me, I heard voices in conversation.

"Then far down the place, in the brighter light of some department which had already raised its blinds, I saw two men approaching. I scrambled to my feet, looking about me for some way of escape, and even as I did so the sound of my movement made them aware of me. I suppose they saw merely a figure moving quietly and quickly away. 'Who's that?' cried one, and 'Stop there!' shouted the other. I dashed round a corner and came full tilt – a faceless figure, mind you! – on a lanky lad of fifteen. He yelled and I bowled him over, rushed past him, turned another corner, and by a happy inspiration threw myself flat behind a counter. In another moment feet went running past and I heard voices shouting, 'All hands to the doors!' asking what was 'up', and giving one another advice how to catch me.

"Lying on the ground, I felt scared out of my wits. But – odd as it may seem – it did not occur to me at the moment to take off my clothes as I should have done. I had made up my mind, I suppose, to get away in them, and that ruled me. And then down the vista of the counters came a bawling of 'Here he is!'

"I sprang to my feet, whipped a chair off the counter and sent it whirling at the fool who had shouted, turned, came into another round a corner, sent him spinning and rushed up the stairs. He kept his footing, gave a view hallo* and came up the staircase hot after me. Up the staircase were piled a multitude of those bright-coloured pot things – what are they?"

"Art pots," suggested Kemp.

"That's it! Art pots. Well, I turned at the top step and swung round, plucked one out of a pile and smashed it on his silly head as he came at me. The whole pile of pots went headlong, and I heard shouting and footsteps running from all parts. I made a mad rush for the refreshment place, and there was a man in white like a man cook, who took up the chase. I made one last desperate turn and found myself among lamps and ironmongery. I went behind the counter of this and waited for my cook, and as he bolted in at the head of the chase I doubled him up with a lamp. Down he went, and I crouched behind the counter and began whipping off my clothes as fast as I could. Coat, jacket, trousers, shoes were all right, but a lambswool vest fits a man like a skin. I heard more men coming, my cook was lying quiet on the other side of the counter, stunned or scared speechless, and I had to make another dash for it, like a rabbit hunted out of a woodpile.

"'This way, policeman!' I heard someone shouting. I found myself in my bedstead storeroom again, and at the end a wilderness of wardrobes. I rushed among them, went flat, got rid of my vest after infinite wriggling and stood a free man again, panting and scared, as the policeman and three of the shopmen came round the corner. They made a rush for the vest and pants and collared the trousers. 'He's dropping his plunder,' said one of the young men. 'He *must* be somewhere here.'

"But they did not find me all the same.

"I stood watching them hunt for me for a time, and cursing my ill luck in losing the clothes. Then I went into the refreshment room, drank a little milk I found there and sat down by the fire to consider my position.

"In a little while two assistants came in and began to talk over the business very excitedly and like the fools they were. I heard a magnified account of my depredations, and other speculations as to my whereabouts. Then I fell to scheming again. The insurmountable difficulty of the place, especially now it was alarmed, was to get any plunder out of it. I went down into the warehouse to see if there was any chance of packing and addressing a parcel, but I could not understand the system of checking. About eleven o'clock, the snow having thawed as it fell, and the day being finer and a little warmer than the previous one, I decided that the emporium was hopeless and went out again, exasperated at my want of success, with only the vaguest plans of action in my mind."

23

In Drury Lane

"BUT YOU BEGIN TO REALIZE NOW," said the Invisible Man, "the full disadvantage of my condition. I had no shelter, no covering. To get clothing was to forgo all my advantage, to make of myself a strange and terrible thing. I was fasting; for to eat, to fill myself with unassimilated matter, would be to become grotesquely visible again."

"I never thought of that," said Kemp.

"Nor had I. And the snow had warned me of other dangers. I could not go abroad in snow – it would settle on me and expose me. Rain, too, would make me a watery outline, a glistening surface of a man – a bubble. And fog – I should be like a fainter bubble in a fog, a surface, a greasy glimmer of humanity. Moreover, as I went abroad – in the London air – I gathered dirt about my ankles, floating smuts and dust upon my skin. I did not know how long it would be before I should become visible from that cause also. But I saw clearly it could not be for long."

"Not in London at any rate."

"I went into the slums towards Great Portland Street, and found myself at the end of the street in which I had lodged. I did not go that way, because of the crowd halfway down it opposite to the still-smoking ruins of the house I had fired. My most immediate problem was to get clothing. What to do with my face puzzled me. Then I saw in one of those little miscellaneous shops – news, sweets, toys, stationery, belated Christmas tomfoolery and so forth – an array of masks and noses. I realized that problem was solved. In a flash I saw my course. I turned about, no longer aimless, and went – circuitously in order to avoid the busy ways – towards the back streets north of the Strand; for I remembered, though not very distinctly where, that some theatrical costumiers had shops in that district.

"The day was cold, with a nipping wind down the northward-running streets. I walked fast to avoid being overtaken. Every crossing was a danger, every passenger a thing to watch alertly. One man, as I was about to pass him at the top of Bedford Street, turned upon me abruptly and came into me, sending me into the road and almost under the wheel of a passing hansom. The verdict of the cab rank was that he had had some sort of stroke. I was so unnerved by this encounter that I went into Covent Garden Market and sat down for some time in a quiet corner by a stall of violets, panting and trembling. I found I had caught a fresh cold, and had to turn out after a time lest my sneezes should attract attention.

"At last I reached the object of my quest, a dirty fly-blown little shop in a byway near Drury Lane, with a window full of tinsel robes, sham jewels, wigs, slippers, dominoes* and theatrical photographs. The shop was old-fashioned and low and dark, and the house rose above it for four storeys, dark and dismal. I peered through the window and, seeing no one within, entered. The opening of the door set a clanking bell ringing. I left it open and walked round a bare costume stand, into a corner behind a cheval glass.* For a minute or so no one came. Then I heard heavy feet striding across a room, and a man appeared down the shop.

"My plans were now perfectly definite. I proposed to make my way into the house, secrete myself upstairs, watch my opportunity and, when everything was quiet, rummage out a wig, mask, spectacles and costume, and go into the world, perhaps a grotesque but still a credible figure. And incidentally of course I could rob the house of any available money.

"The man who had entered the shop was a short, slightly hunched, beetle-browed man, with long arms and very short bandy legs. Apparently I had interrupted a meal. He stared about the shop with an expression of expectation. This gave way to surprise, and then anger, as he saw the shop empty. 'Damn the boys!' he said. He went to stare up and down the street. He came in again in a minute, kicked the door to with his foot spitefully, and went muttering back to the house door.

"I came forward to follow him, and at the noise of my movement he stopped dead. I did so too, startled by his quickness of ear. He slammed the house door in my face.

"I stood hesitating. Suddenly I heard his quick footsteps returning, and the door reopened. He stood looking about the shop like one who was still not satisfied. Then, murmuring to himself, he examined the back of the counter and peered behind some fixtures. Then he stood doubtful. He had left the house door open and I slipped into the inner room.

"It was a queer little room, poorly furnished and with a number of big masks in the corner. On the table was his belated breakfast, and it was a confoundedly exasperating thing for me, Kemp, to have to sniff his coffee and stand watching while he came in and resumed his meal. And his table manners were irritating. Three doors opened into the little room, one going upstairs and one down, but they were all shut. I could not get out of the room while he was there, I could scarcely move because of his alertness and there was a draught down my back. Twice I strangled a sneeze just in time.

"The spectacular quality of my sensations was curious and novel, but for all that I was heartily tired and angry long before he had done his eating. But at last he made an end and, putting his beggarly crockery on the black tin tray upon which he had had his teapot and gathering all the crumbs up on the mustard-stained cloth, he took the whole lot of things after him. His burden prevented his shutting the door behind him – as he would have done: I never saw such a man for shutting doors – and I followed him into a very dirty underground kitchen and scullery. I had the pleasure of seeing him begin to wash up, and then, finding no good in keeping down there, and the brick floor being cold to my feet, I returned upstairs and sat in his chair by the fire. It was burning low and, scarcely thinking, I put on a little coal. The noise of this brought him up at once, and he stood aglare. He peered about the room and was within an ace of touching me. Even after that examination, he scarcely seemed satisfied. He stopped in the doorway and took a final inspection before he went down.

"I waited in the little parlour for an age, and at last he came up and opened the upstairs door. I just managed to get by him.

"On the staircase he stopped suddenly, so that I very nearly blundered into him. He stood looking back right into my face and listening. 'I could have sworn,' he said. His long hairy hand pulled at his lower lip. His eye went up and down the staircase. Then he grunted and went on up again.

"His hand was on the handle of a door, and then he stopped again with the same puzzled anger on his face. He was becoming aware of the faint sounds of my movements about him. The man must have had diabolically acute hearing. He suddenly flashed into rage. 'If there's anyone in this house,' he cried with an oath, and left the threat unfinished. He put his hand in his pocket, failed to find what he wanted and, rushing past me, went blundering noisily and pugnaciously downstairs. But I did not follow him. I sat on the head of the staircase until his return.

"Presently he came up again, still muttering. He opened the door of the room and, before I could enter, slammed it in my face.

"I resolved to explore the house, and spent some time in doing so as noiselessly as possible. The house was very old and tumbledown, damp so that the paper in the attics was peeling from the walls and rat-infested. Some of the door handles were stiff and I was afraid to turn them. Several rooms I did inspect were unfurnished, and others were littered with theatrical lumber, bought second-hand, I judged, from its appearance. In one room next to his I found a lot of old clothes. I began routing among these, and in my eagerness forgot again the evident sharpness of his ears. I heard a stealthy footstep and, looking up just in time, saw him peering in at the tumbled heap and holding an old-fashioned revolver in his hand. I stood perfectly still while he stared about open-mouthed and suspicious. 'It must have been her,' he said slowly. 'Damn her!'

"He shut the door quietly, and immediately I heard the key turn in the lock. Then his footsteps retreated. I realized abruptly that I was locked in. For a minute I did not know what to do. I walked from door to window and back, and stood perplexed. A gust of anger came upon me. But I decided to inspect the clothes before I did anything further, and my first attempt brought down a pile from an upper shelf. This brought him back, more sinister than ever. That time he actually touched me, jumped back with amazement and stood astonished in the middle of the room.

"Presently he calmed a little. 'Rats,' he said in an undertone, fingers on lip. He was evidently a little scared. I edged quietly out of the room, but a plank creaked. Then the infernal little brute started going all over the house, revolver in hand and locking door after door and pocketing the keys. When I realized what he was up to I had a fit of rage – I could hardly control myself sufficiently to watch my opportunity. By this time I knew he was alone in the house, and so I made no more ado, but knocked him on the head."

"Knocked him on the head!" exclaimed Kemp.

"Yes – stunned him – as he was going downstairs. Hit him from behind with a stool that stood on the landing. He went downstairs like a bag of old boots."

"But!... I say! The common conventions of humanity—"

"Are all very well for common people. But the point was, Kemp, that I had to get out of that house in a disguise without his seeing me. I couldn't think of any other way of doing it. And then I gagged him with a Louis Quatorze vest* and tied him up in a sheet."

"Tied him up in a sheet!"

"Made a sort of bag of it. It was rather a good idea to keep the idiot scared and quiet, and a devilish hard thing to get out of – head away from the string. My dear Kemp, it's no good your sitting and glaring as though I was a murderer. It had to be done. He had his revolver. If once he saw me he would be able to describe me—"

"But still," said Kemp, "in England – today. And the man was in his own house, and you were – well, robbing."

"Robbing! Confound it! You'll call me a thief next! Surely, Kemp, you're not fool enough to dance on the old strings. Can't you see my position?"

"And his too," said Kemp.

The Invisible Man stood up sharply. "What do you mean to say?"

Kemp's face grew a trifle hard. He was about to speak and checked himself. "I suppose, after all," he said with a sudden change of manner, "the thing had to be done. You were in a fix. But still—"

"Of course I was in a fix – an infernal fix. And he made me wild too – hunting me about the house, fooling about with his revolver, locking and unlocking doors. He was simply exasperating. You don't blame me, do you? You don't blame me?"

"I never blame anyone," said Kemp. "It's quite out of fashion. What did you do next?"

"I was hungry. Downstairs I found a loaf and some rank cheese – more than sufficient to satisfy my hunger. I took some brandy and water, and then went up past my impromptu bag – he was lying quite still – to the room containing the old clothes. This looked out upon the street, two lace curtains brown with dirt guarding the window. I went and peered out through their interstices. Outside the day was bright – by contrast with the brown shadows of the dismal house in which I found myself, dazzlingly bright. A brisk traffic was going by, fruit carts, a hansom, a four-wheeler with a pile of boxes, a fishmonger's cart. I turned with spots of colour swimming before my eyes to the shadowy fixtures behind me. My excitement was giving place to a clear apprehension of my position again. The room was full of a faint scent of benzoline* – used, I suppose, in cleaning the garments.

"I began a systematic search of the place. I should judge the hunchback had been alone in the house for some time. He was a curious person. Everything that could possibly be of service to me I collected in the clothes storeroom, and then I made a deliberate selection. I found a handbag I thought a suitable possession, and some powder, rouge and sticking plaster.

"I had thought of painting and powdering my face and all that there was to show of me, in order to render myself visible, but the disadvantage of this lay in the fact that I should require turpentine and other appliances and a considerable amount of time before I could vanish again. Finally I chose a mask of the better type, slightly grotesque but not more so than many human beings, dark glasses, greyish whiskers and a wig. I could find no underclothing, but that I could buy subsequently, and for the time I swathed myself in calico dominoes and some white cashmere scarves. I could find no socks, but the hunchback's boots were rather a loose fit and sufficed. In a desk in the shop were three sovereigns and about thirty shillings' worth of silver, and in a locked cupboard I burst in the inner room were eight pounds in gold. I could go forth into the world again, equipped.

"Then came a curious hesitation. Was my appearance really – credible? I tried myself with a little bedroom looking glass, inspecting myself from every point of view to discover any forgotten chink, but it all seemed sound. I was grotesque to the theatrical pitch, a stage miser, but I was certainly not a physical impossibility. Gathering confidence, I took my looking glass down into the shop, pulled down the shop blinds and surveyed myself from every point of view with the help of the cheval glass in the corner.

"I spent some minutes screwing up my courage and then unlocked the shop door and marched out into the street, leaving the little man to get out of his sheet again when he liked. In five minutes a dozen turnings intervened between me and the costumier's shop. No one appeared to notice me very pointedly. My last difficulty seemed overcome."

He stopped again.

"And you troubled no more about the hunchback?" said Kemp.

"No," said the Invisible Man. "Nor have I heard what became of him. I suppose he untied himself or kicked himself out. The knots were pretty tight."

He became silent, and went to the window and stared out.

"What happened when you went out into the Strand?"

"Oh! Disillusionment again. I thought my troubles were over. Practically I thought I had impunity to do whatever I chose, everything – save to give away my secret. So I thought. Whatever I did, whatever the consequences might be, was nothing to me. I had merely to fling aside my garments and vanish. No person could hold me. I could take my money where I found it. I decided to treat myself to a sumptuous feast, and then put up at a good hotel, and accumulate a new outfit of property. I felt amazingly confident – it's not particularly pleasant recalling that I was an ass. I went into a place and was already ordering a lunch, when it occurred to me that I could not eat unless I exposed my invisible face. I finished ordering the lunch, told the man I should be back in ten minutes, and went out exasperated. I don't know if you have ever been disappointed in your appetite."

"Not quite so badly," said Kemp, "but I can imagine it."

"I could have smashed the silly devils. At last, faint with the desire for tasteful food, I went into another place and demanded a private room. 'I am disfigured,' I said. 'Badly.' They looked at me curiously, but of course it was not their affair – and so at last I got my lunch. It was not particularly well served, but it sufficed; and when I had had it, I sat over a cigar, trying to plan my line of action. And outside a snowstorm was beginning.

"The more I thought it over, Kemp, the more I realized what a helpless absurdity an invisible man was – in a cold and dirty climate and a crowded, civilized city. Before I made this mad experiment I had dreamt of a thousand advantages. That afternoon it seemed all disappointment. I went over the heads of the things a man reckons desirable. No doubt invisibility made it possible to get them, but it made it impossible to enjoy them when they are got. Ambition – what is the good of pride of place when you cannot appear there? What is the good of the love of woman when her name must needs be Delilah?* I have no taste for politics, for the blackguardisms of fame, for philanthropy, for sport. What was I to do? And for this I had become a wrapped-up mystery, a swathed and bandaged caricature of a man!"

He paused, and his attitude suggested a roving glance at the window.

"But how did you get to Iping?" said Kemp, anxious to keep his guest busy talking.

"I went there to work. I had one hope. It was a half-idea! I have it still. It is a full-blown idea now. A way of getting back! Of restoring what I have done. When I choose. When I have done all I mean to do invisibly. And that is what I chiefly want to talk to you about now."

"You went straight to Iping?"

"Yes. I had simply to get my three volumes of memoranda and my chequebook, my luggage and underclothing, order a quantity of chemicals to work out this idea of mine – I will show you the calculations as soon as I get my books – and then I started. Jove! I remember the snowstorm now, and the accursed bother it was to keep the snow from damping my pasteboard nose."

"At the end," said Kemp, "the day before yesterday, when they found you out, you rather – to judge by the papers—"

"I did. Rather. Did I kill that fool of a constable?"

"No," said Kemp. "He's expected to recover."

"That's his luck, then. I clean lost my temper, the fools! Why couldn't they leave me alone? And that grocer lout?"

"There are no deaths expected," said Kemp.

"I don't know about that tramp of mine," said the Invisible Man, with an unpleasant laugh.

"By Heaven, Kemp, you don't know what rage *is*! To have worked for years, to have planned and plotted, and then to get some fumbling purblind idiot messing across your course! Every conceivable sort of silly creature that has ever been created has been sent to cross me.

"If I have much more of it, I shall go wild – I shall start mowing 'em.

"As it is, they've made things a thousand times more difficult."

"No doubt it's exasperating," said Kemp drily.

24

The Plan That Failed

"BUT NOW," SAID KEMP, with a side glance out of the window, "what are we to do?"

He moved nearer his guest as he spoke in such a manner as to prevent the possibility of a glimpse of the three men who were advancing up the hill road – with an intolerable slowness, as it seemed to Kemp.

"What were you planning to do when you were heading for Port Burdock? *Had* you any plan?"

"I was going to clear out of the country. But I have altered that plan rather since seeing you. I thought it would be wise, now the weather is hot and invisibility possible, to make for the south. Especially as my secret was known, and everyone would be on the lookout for a masked and muffled man. You have a line of steamers from here to France. My idea was to get aboard one and run the risks of the passage. Thence I could go by train into Spain, or else get to Algiers. It would not be difficult. There a man might always be invisible – and yet live. And do things. I was using that tramp as a money box and luggage carrier, until I decided how to get my books and things sent over to meet me."

"That's clear."

"And then the filthy brute must needs try and rob me! He has hidden my books, Kemp. Hidden my books! If I can lay my hands on him!"

"Best plan to get the books out of him first."

"But where is he? Do you know?"

"He's in the town police station, locked up, by his own request, in the strongest cell in the place."

"Cur!" said the Invisible Man.

"But that hangs up your plans a little."

"We must get those books – those books are vital."

"Certainly," said Kemp, a little nervously, wondering if he heard footsteps outside. "Certainly we must get those books. But that won't be difficult, if he doesn't know they're for you."

"No," said the Invisible Man, and thought.

Kemp tried to think of something to keep the talk going, but the Invisible Man resumed of his own accord.

"Blundering into your house, Kemp," he said, "changes all my plans. For you are a man that can understand. In spite of all that has happened, in spite of this publicity, of the loss of my books, of what I have suffered, there still remain great possibilities, huge possibilities...

"You have told no one I am here?" he asked abruptly.

Kemp hesitated. "That was implied," he said.

"No one?" insisted Griffin.

"Not a soul."

"Ah! Now..." The Invisible Man stood up, and sticking his arms akimbo began to pace the study.

"I made a mistake, Kemp, a huge mistake, in carrying this thing through alone. I have wasted strength, time, opportunities. Alone – it is wonderful how little a man can do alone! To rob a little, to hurt a little, and there is the end.

"What I want, Kemp, is a goalkeeper, a helper and a hiding place, an arrangement whereby I can sleep and eat and rest in peace, and unsuspected. I must have a confederate. With a confederate, with food and rest – a thousand things are possible.

"Hitherto I have gone on vague lines. We have to consider all that invisibility means, all that it does not mean. It means little advantage for eavesdropping and so forth – one makes sounds. It's of little help, a little help perhaps – in housebreaking and so forth. Once you've caught me you could easily imprison me. But on the other hand I am hard to catch. This invisibility, in fact, is only good in two cases: it's useful in getting away, it's useful in approaching. It's particularly useful, therefore, in killing. I can walk round a man, whatever weapon he has, choose my point, strike as I like. Dodge as I like. Escape as I like."

Kemp's hand went to his moustache. Was that a movement downstairs?

"And it is killing we must do, Kemp."

"It is killing we must do," repeated Kemp. "I'm listening to your plan, Griffin, but I'm not agreeing, mind. *Why* killing?"

"Not wanton killing, but a judicious slaying. The point is, they know there is an invisible man – as well as we know there is an invisible man. And that invisible man, Kemp, must now establish a Reign of Terror.* Yes – no doubt it's startling. But I mean it. A Reign of Terror. He must take some town like your Burdock and terrify and dominate it. He must issue his orders. He can do that in a thousand ways – scraps of paper thrust under doors would suffice. And all who disobey his orders he must kill, and kill all who would defend the disobedient."

"Humph!" said Kemp, no longer listening to Griffin but to the sound of his front door opening and closing.

"It seems to me, Griffin," he said, to cover his wandering attention, "that your confederate would be in a difficult position."

"No one would know he was a confederate," said the Invisible Man eagerly. And then suddenly, "*Hush!* What's that downstairs?"

"Nothing," said Kemp, and suddenly began to speak loud and fast. "I don't agree to this, Griffin," he said. "Understand me, I don't agree to this. Why dream of playing a game against the race? How can you hope to gain happiness? Don't be a lone wolf. Publish your results; take the world – take the nation at least – into your confidence. Think what you might do with a million helpers—"

The Invisible Man interrupted Kemp. "There are footsteps coming upstairs," he said in a low voice.

"Nonsense," said Kemp.

"Let me see," said the Invisible Man, and advanced, arm extended, to the door.

Kemp hesitated for a second and then moved to intercept him. The Invisible Man started and stood still. "Traitor!" cried the Voice, and suddenly the dressing gown opened and, sitting down, the Unseen began to disrobe. Kemp made three swift steps to the door, and forthwith the Invisible Man – his legs had vanished – sprang to his feet with a shout. Kemp flung the door open.

As it opened, there came a sound of hurrying feet downstairs and voices.

With a quick movement Kemp thrust the Invisible Man back, sprang aside, and slammed the door. The key was outside and ready. In another moment Griffin would have been alone in the belvedere study, a prisoner. Save for one little thing. The key had been slipped in hastily that morning. As Kemp slammed the door it fell noisily upon the carpet.

Kemp's face became white. He tried to grip the door handle with both hands. For a moment he stood lugging. Then the door gave six inches. But he got it closed again. The second time it was jerked a foot wide, and the dressing gown came wedging itself into the opening. His throat was gripped by invisible fingers, and he left his hold on the handle to defend himself. He was forced back, tripped and pitched heavily into the corner of the landing. The empty dressing gown was flung on the top of him.

Halfway up the staircase was Colonel Adye, the recipient of Kemp's letter, the chief of the Burdock police. He was staring aghast at the sudden appearance of Kemp, followed by the extraordinary sight of clothing tossing empty in the air. He saw Kemp felled, and struggling to his feet. He saw Kemp reel, rush forward and go down again, felled like an ox.

Then suddenly he was struck violently. By nothing! A vast weight, it seemed, leapt upon him, and he was hurled headlong down the staircase, with a grip at his throat and a knee in his groin. An invisible foot trod on his back, a ghostly patter passed downstairs, he heard the two police officers in the hall shout and run, and the front door of the house slammed violently.

He rolled over and sat up staring. He saw, staggering down the staircase, Kemp, dusty and dishevelled, one side of his face white from a blow, his lip bleeding, holding a pink dressing gown and some underclothing in his arms.

"My God!" cried Kemp. "The game's up! He's gone!"

25

The Hunting of the Invisible Man

FOR A SPACE KEMP WAS TOO INARTICULATE to make Adye understand the swift things that had just happened. The two men stood on the landing, Kemp speaking swiftly, the grotesque swathings of Griffin still on his arm. But presently Adye began to grasp something of the situation.

"He is mad," said Kemp, "inhuman. He is pure selfishness. He thinks of nothing but his own advantage, his own safety. I have listened to such a story this morning of brutal self-seeking! He has wounded men. He will kill them unless we can prevent him. He will create a panic. Nothing can stop him. He is going out now – furious!"

"He must be caught," said Adye. "That is certain."

"But how?" cried Kemp, and suddenly became full of ideas.

"You must begin at once. You must set every available man to work. You must prevent his leaving this district. Once he gets away, he may go through the countryside as he wills, kill-ing and maiming. He dreams of a Reign of Terror! A Reign of Terror, I tell you. You must set a watch on trains and roads and shipping. The garrison must help. You must wire for help. The only thing that may keep him here is the thought of recovering some books of notes he counts of value. I will tell you of that! There is a man in your police station – Marvel."

"I know," said Adye, "I know. Those books – yes."

"And you must prevent him from eating or sleeping; day and night the country must be astir for him. Food must be locked up and secured, all food, so that he will have to break his way to it. The houses everywhere must be barred against him. Heaven send us cold nights and rain! The whole countryside must begin hunting and keep hunting. I tell you, Adye, he is a danger, a disaster; unless he is pinned and secured, it is frightful to think of the things that may happen."

"What else can we do?" said Adye. "I must go down at once and begin organizing. But why not come? Yes – you come too! Come, and we must hold a sort of council of war – get Hopps to help – and the railway managers. By Jove! It's urgent. Come along – tell me as we go. What else is there we can do? Put that stuff down."

In another moment Adye was leading the way downstairs. They found the front door open and the policemen standing outside staring at empty air. "He's got away, sir," said one.

"We must go to the central station at once," said Adye. "One of you go on down and get a cab to come up and meet us – quickly. And now, Kemp, what else?"

"Dogs," said Kemp. "Get dogs. They don't see him, but they wind him. Get dogs."

"Good," said Adye. "It's not generally known, but the prison officials over at Halstead know a man with bloodhounds. Dogs. What else?"

"Bear in mind," said Kemp, "his food shows. After eating, his food shows until it is assimilated. So that he has to hide after eating. You must keep on beating – every thicket, every quiet corner. And put all weapons, all implements that might be weapons, away. He can't carry such things for long. And what he can snatch up and strike men with must be hidden away."

CHAPTER 25

"Good again," said Adye. "We shall have him yet!"

"And on the roads," said Kemp, and hesitated.

"Yes?" said Adye.

"Powdered glass," said Kemp. "It's cruel, I know. But think of what he may do!"

Adye drew the air in between his teeth sharply. "It's unsportsmanlike. I don't know. But I'll have powdered glass got ready. If he goes too far—"

"The man's become inhuman, I tell you," said Kemp. "I am as sure he will establish a Reign of Terror – so soon as he has got over the emotions of this escape – as I am sure I am talking to you. Our only chance is to be ahead. He has cut himself off from his kind. His blood be upon his own head."

26

The Wicksteed Murder

T HE INVISIBLE MAN SEEMS to have rushed out of Kemp's
house in a state of blind fury. A little child playing near
Kemp's gateway was violently caught up and thrown aside,
so that its ankle was broken, and thereafter for some hours
the Invisible Man passed out of human perceptions. No one
knows where he went nor what he did. But one can imagine
him hurrying through the hot June forenoon, up the hill and
on to the open down land behind Port Burdock, raging and
despairing at his intolerable fate, and sheltering at last, heated
and weary, amid the thickets of Hintondean, to piece together
again his shattered schemes against his species. That seems the
most probable refuge for him, for there it was he reasserted
himself in a grimly tragical manner about two in the afternoon.

One wonders what his state of mind may have been during
that time, and what plans he devised. No doubt he was almost
ecstatically exasperated by Kemp's treachery, and though we
may be able to understand the motives that led to that deceit, we
may still imagine and even sympathize a little with the fury the
attempted surprise must have occasioned. Perhaps something of
the stunned astonishment of his Oxford Street experiences may
have returned to him, for evidently he had counted on Kemp's
cooperation in his brutal dream of a terrorized world. At any rate
he vanished from human ken about midday, and no living witness

can tell what he did until about half-past two. It was a fortunate thing, perhaps, for humanity, but for him it was a fatal inaction.

During that time a growing multitude of men scattered over the countryside were busy. In the morning he had still been simply a legend, a terror; in the afternoon, by virtue chiefly of Kemp's drily worded proclamation, he was presented as a tangible antagonist, to be wounded, captured or overcome, and the countryside began organizing itself with inconceivable rapidity. By two o'clock even he might still have removed himself out of the district by getting aboard a train, but after two that became impossible. Every passenger train along the lines on a great parallelogram between Southampton, Winchester, Brighton and Horsham travelled with locked doors, and the goods traffic was almost entirely suspended. And in a great circle of twenty miles round Port Burdock, men armed with guns and bludgeons were presently setting out in groups of three and four, with dogs, to beat the roads and fields.

Mounted policemen rode along the country lanes, stopping at every cottage and warning the people to lock up their houses and keep indoors unless they were armed, and all the elementary schools had broken up by three o'clock, and the children, scared and keeping together in groups, were hurrying home. Kemp's proclamation – signed indeed by Adye – was posted over almost the whole district by four or five o'clock in the afternoon. It gave briefly but clearly all the conditions of the struggle, the necessity of keeping the Invisible Man from food and sleep, the necessity for incessant watchfulness and for a prompt attention to any evidence of his movements. And so swift and decided was the action of the authorities, so prompt and universal was the belief in this strange being, that before nightfall an area of several hundred square miles was in a stringent state of siege. And before nightfall, too, a thrill of horror went through the whole watching nervous countryside. Going from whispering mouth to mouth, swift and certain over the length and breadth of the county, passed the story of the murder of Mr Wicksteed.

If our supposition that the Invisible Man's refuge was the Hintondean thickets is correct, then we must suppose that in the early afternoon he sallied out again, bent upon some project that involved the use of a weapon. We cannot know what the project was, but the evidence that he had the iron rod in hand before he met Wicksteed is to me at least overwhelming.

We can know nothing of the details of the encounter. It occurred on the edge of a gravel pit, not two hundred yards from Lord Burdock's lodge gate. Everything points to a desperate struggle – the trampled ground, the numerous wounds Mr Wicksteed received, his splintered walking stick; but why the attack was made – save in a murderous frenzy – it is impossible to imagine. Indeed, the theory of madness is almost unavoidable. Mr Wicksteed was a man of forty-five or forty-six, steward to Lord Burdock, of inoffensive habits and appearance, the very last person in the world to provoke such a terrible antagonist. Against him it would seem the Invisible Man used an iron rod dragged from a broken piece of fence. He stopped this quiet man, going quietly home to his midday meal, attacked him, beat down his feeble defences, broke his arm, felled him and smashed his head to a jelly.

He must have dragged this rod out of the fencing before he met his victim; he must have been carrying it ready in his hand. Only two details beyond what has already been stated seem to bear on the matter. One is the circumstance that the gravel pit was not in Mr Wicksteed's direct path home, but nearly a couple of hundred yards out of his way. The other is the assertion of a little girl to the effect that, going to her afternoon school, she saw the murdered man "trotting" in a peculiar manner across a field towards the gravel pit. Her pantomime of his action suggests a man pursuing something on the ground before him and striking at it ever and again with his walking stick. She was the last person to see him alive. He passed out of her sight to his death, the struggle being hidden from her only by a clump of beech trees and a slight depression in the ground.

Now this, to the present writer's mind at least, lifts the murder out of the realm of the absolutely wanton. We may imagine that Griffin had taken the rod as a weapon indeed, but without any deliberate intention of using it in murder. Wicksteed may then have come by and noticed this rod inexplicably moving through the air. Without any thought of the Invisible Man – for Port Burdock is ten miles away – he may have pursued it. It is quite conceivable that he may not even have heard of the Invisible Man. One can then imagine the Invisible Man making off – quietly in order to avoid discovering his presence in the neighbourhood, and Wicksteed, excited and curious, pursuing this unaccountably locomotive object – finally striking at it.

No doubt the Invisible Man could easily have distanced his middle-aged pursuer under ordinary circumstances, but the position in which Wicksteed's body was found suggests that he had the ill luck to drive his quarry into a corner between a drift of stinging nettles and the gravel pit. To those who appreciate the extraordinary irascibility of the Invisible Man, the rest of the encounter will be easy to imagine.

But this is pure hypothesis. The only undeniable facts – for stories of children are often unreliable – are the discovery of Wicksteed's body, done to death, and of the bloodstained iron rod flung among the nettles. The abandonment of the rod by Griffin suggests that in the emotional excitement of the affair, the purpose for which he took it – if he had a purpose – was abandoned. He was certainly an intensely egotistical and unfeeling man, but the sight of his victim, his first victim, bloody and pitiful at his feet, may have released some long pent fountain of remorse to flood for a time whatever scheme of action he had contrived.

After the murder of Mr Wicksteed, he would seem to have struck across the country towards the downland. There is a story of a voice heard about sunset by a couple of men in a field near Fern Bottom. It was wailing and laughing, sobbing and groaning, and ever and again it shouted. It must have been queer hearing. It drove up across the middle of a clover field and died away towards the hills.

That afternoon the Invisible Man must have learnt something of the rapid use Kemp had made of his confidences. He must have found houses locked and secured; he may have loitered about railway stations and prowled about inns, and no doubt he read the proclamations and realized something of the nature of the campaign against him. And as the evening advanced, the field became dotted here and there with groups of three or four men, and noisy with the yelping of dogs. These men-hunters had particular instructions as to the way they should support one another in the case of an encounter. He avoided them all. We may understand something of his exasperation, and it could have been none the less because he himself had supplied the information that was being used so remorselessly against him. For that day at least he lost heart; for nearly twenty-four hours, save when he turned on Wicksteed, he was a hunted man. In the night, he must have eaten and slept; for in the morning he was himself again, active, powerful, angry and malignant, prepared for his last great struggle against the world.

27

The Siege of Kemp's House

K EMP READ A STRANGE MISSIVE, written in pencil on a greasy sheet of paper.

"You have been amazingly energetic and clever," this letter ran, "though what you stand to gain by it I cannot imagine. You are against me. For a whole day you have chased me; you have tried to rob me of a night's rest. But I have had food in spite of you, I have slept in spite of you, and the game is only beginning. The game is only beginning. There is nothing for it, but to start the Terror. This announces the first day of the Terror. Port Burdock is no longer under the Queen, tell your colonel of police, and the rest of them; it is under me – the Terror! This is day one of year one of the new epoch – the Epoch of the Invisible Man. I am Invisible Man the First. To begin with the rule will be easy. The first day there will be one execution for the sake of example – a man named Kemp. Death starts for him today. He may lock himself away, hide himself away, get guards about him, put on armour if he likes: Death, the unseen Death, is coming. Let him take precautions; it will impress my people. Death starts from the pillar box by midday. The letter will fall in as the postman comes along, then off! The game begins. Death starts. Help him not, my people, lest Death fall upon you also. Today Kemp is to die."

Kemp read this letter twice. "It's no hoax," he said. "That's his voice! And he means it."

He turned the folded sheet over and saw on the addressed side of it the postmark Hintondean, and the prosaic detail "2d to pay".

He got up, leaving his lunch unfinished – the letter had come by the one-o'clock post – and went into his study. He rang for his housekeeper, and told her to go round the house at once, examine all the fastenings of the windows and close all the shutters. He closed the shutters of his study himself. From a locked drawer in his bedroom he took a little revolver, examined it carefully and put it into the pocket of his lounge jacket. He wrote a number of brief notes, one to Colonel Adye, gave them to his servant to take, with explicit instructions as to her way of leaving the house. "There is no danger," he said, and added a mental reservation, "to you." He remained meditative for a space after doing this, and then returned to his cooling lunch.

He ate with gaps of thought. Finally he struck the table sharply. "We will have him!" he said. "And I am the bait. He will come too far."

He went up to the belvedere, carefully shutting every door after him. "It's a game," he said, "an odd game – but the chances are all for me, Mr Griffin, in spite of your invisibility. Griffin *contra mundum** – with a vengeance!"

He stood at the window staring at the hot hillside. "He must get food every day – and I don't envy him. Did he really sleep last night? Out in the open somewhere – secure from collisions. I wish we could get some good cold wet weather instead of the heat.

"He may be watching me now."

He went close to the window. Something rapped smartly against the brickwork over the frame, and made him start violently.

"I'm getting nervous," said Kemp. But it was five minutes before he went to the window again. "It must have been a sparrow," he said.

Presently he heard the front doorbell ringing, and hurried downstairs. He unbolted and unlocked the door, examined the chain, put it up and opened cautiously without showing himself. A familiar voice hailed him. It was Adye.

"Your servant's been assaulted, Kemp," he said round the door.

"What!" exclaimed Kemp.

"Had that note of yours taken away from her. He's close about here. Let me in."

Kemp released the chain, and Adye entered through as narrow an opening as possible. He stood in the hall, looking with infinite relief at Kemp refastening the door. "Note was snatched out of her hand. Scared her horribly. She's down at the station. Hysterics. He's close here. What was it about?"

Kemp swore.

"What a fool I was," said Kemp. "I might have known. It's not an hour's walk from Hintondean. Already!"

"What's up?" said Adye.

"Look here!" said Kemp, and led the way into his study. He handed Adye the Invisible Man's letter. Adye read it and whistled softly. "And you?..." said Adye.

"Proposed a trap – like a fool," said Kemp, "and sent my proposal out by a maidservant. To him."

Adye followed Kemp's profanity.

"He'll clear out," said Adye.

"Not he," said Kemp.

A resounding smash of glass came from upstairs. Adye had a silvery glimpse of a little revolver half out of Kemp's pocket. "It's a window, upstairs!" said Kemp, and led the way up. There came a second smash while they were still on the staircase. When they reached the study they found two of the three windows smashed, half the room littered with splintered glass and one big flint lying on the writing table. The two men stopped in the doorway, contemplating the wreckage. Kemp swore again, and as he did so the third window went with a snap like a pistol, hung starred for a moment and collapsed in jagged, shivering triangles into the room.

"What's this for?" said Adye.

"It's a beginning," said Kemp.

"There's no way of climbing up here?"

"Not for a cat," said Kemp.

"No shutters?"

"Not here. All the downstairs rooms – hullo!"

Smash, and then whack of boards hit hard came from downstairs. "Confound him!" said Kemp. "That must be – yes – it's one of the bedrooms. He's going to do all the house. But he's a fool. The shutters are up, and the glass will fall outside. He'll cut his feet."

Another window proclaimed its destruction. The two men stood on the landing perplexed. "I have it!" said Adye. "Let me have a stick or something, and I'll go down to the station and get the bloodhounds put on. That ought to settle him! They're hard by – not ten minutes—"

Another window went the way of its fellows.

"You haven't a revolver?" asked Adye.

Kemp's hand went to his pocket. Then he hesitated. "I haven't one – at least to spare."

"I'll bring it back," said Adye, "you'll be safe here."

Kemp handed him the weapon.

"Now for the door," said Adye.

As they stood hesitating in the hall, they heard one of the first-floor bedroom windows crack and clash. Kemp went to the door and began to slip the bolts as silently as possible. His face was a little paler than usual. "You must step straight out," said Kemp. In another moment Adye was on the doorstep and the bolts were dropping back into the staples. He hesitated for a moment, feeling more comfortable with his back against the door. Then he marched, upright and square, down the steps. He crossed the lawn and approached the gate. A little breeze seemed to ripple over the grass. Something moved near him. "Stop a bit," said a voice, and Adye stopped dead and his hand tightened on the revolver.

"Well?" said Adye, white and grim, and every nerve tense.

"Oblige me by going back to the house," said the Voice, as tense and grim as Adye's.

"Sorry," said Adye a little hoarsely, and moistened his lips with his tongue. The Voice was on his left front, he thought. Suppose he were to take his luck with a shot?

"What are you going for?" said the Voice, and there was a quick movement of the two, and a flash of sunlight from the open lip of Adye's pocket.

Adye desisted and thought. "Where I go," he said slowly, "is my own business." The words were still on his lips, when an arm came round his neck, his back felt a knee, and he was sprawling backwards. He drew clumsily and fired absurdly, and in another moment he was struck in the mouth and the revolver wrested from his grip. He made a vain clutch at a slippery limb, tried to struggle up and fell back. "Damn!" said Adye. The Voice laughed. "I'd kill you now if it wasn't the waste of a bullet," it said. He saw the revolver in mid-air, six feet off, covering him.

"Well?" said Adye, sitting up.

"Get up," said the Voice.

Adye stood up.

"Attention," said the Voice, and then fiercely: "Don't try any games. Remember I can see your face if you can't see mine. You've got to go back to the house."

"He won't let me in," said Adye.

"That's a pity," said the Invisible Man. "I've got no quarrel with you."

Adye moistened his lips again. He glanced away from the barrel of the revolver and saw the sea far off very blue and dark under the midday sun, the smooth green down, the white cliff of the Head and the multitudinous town, and suddenly he knew that life was very sweet. His eyes came back to this little metal thing hanging between heaven and earth, six yards away. "What am I to do?" he said sullenly.

"What am I to do?" asked the Invisible Man. "You will get help. The only thing is for you to go back."

"I will try. If he lets me in will you promise not to rush the door?"

"I've got no quarrel with you," said the Voice.

Kemp had hurried upstairs after letting Adye out and, now crouching among the broken glass and peering cautiously over the edge of the study window sill, he saw Adye stand parleying with the Unseen. "Why doesn't he fire?" whispered Kemp to himself. Then the revolver moved a little and the glint of the sunlight flashed in Kemp's eyes. He shaded his eyes and tried to see the source of the blinding beam.

"Surely," he said, "Adye has given up the revolver!"

"Promise not to rush the door," Adye was saying. "Don't push a winning game too far. Give a man a chance."

"You go back to the house. I tell you flatly I will not promise anything."

Adye's decision seemed suddenly made. He turned towards the house, walking slowly with his hands behind him. Kemp watched him – puzzled. The revolver vanished, flashed again into sight, vanished again and became evident on a closer scrutiny as a little dark object following Adye. Then things happened very quickly. Adye leapt backwards, swung round, clutched at this little object, missed it, threw up his hands and fell forward on his face, leaving a little puff of blue in the air. Kemp did not hear the sound of the shot. Adye writhed, raised himself on one arm, fell forward and lay still.

For a space Kemp remained staring at the quiet carelessness of Adye's attitude. The afternoon was very hot and still, nothing seemed stirring in all the world save a couple of yellow butterflies chasing each other through the shrubbery between the house and the road gate. Adye lay on the lawn near the gate. The blinds of all the villas down the hill road were drawn, but in one little green summer house was a white figure, apparently an old man asleep. Kemp scrutinized the surroundings of the house for a glimpse of the revolver, but it had vanished. His eyes came back to Adye. The game was opening well.

Then came a ringing and knocking at the front door, that grew at last tumultuous, but pursuant to Kemp's instructions the servants had locked themselves into their rooms. This was followed by a silence. Kemp sat listening and then began peering cautiously out of the three windows, one after another. He went to the staircase head and stood listening uneasily. He armed himself with his bedroom poker and went to examine the interior fastenings of the ground-floor windows again. Everything was safe and quiet. He returned to the belvedere. Adye lay motionless over the edge of the gravel just as he had fallen. Coming along the road by the villas were the housemaid and two policemen.

Everything was deadly still. The three people seemed very slow in approaching. He wondered what his antagonist was doing.

He started. There was a smash from below. He hesitated and went downstairs again. Suddenly the house resounded with heavy blows and the splintering of wood. He heard a smash and the destructive clang of the iron fastenings of the shutters. He turned the key and opened the kitchen door. As he did so, the shutters, split and splintering, came flying inward. He stood aghast. The window frame, save for one crossbar, was still intact, but only little teeth of glass remained in the frame. The shutters had been driven in with an axe, and now the axe was descending in sweeping blows upon the window frame and the iron bars defending it. Then suddenly it leapt aside and vanished. He saw the revolver lying on the path outside, and then the little weapon sprang into the air. He dodged back. The revolver cracked just too late, and a splinter from the edge of the closing door flashed over his head. He slammed and locked the door, and as he stood outside he heard Griffin shouting and laughing. Then the blows of the axe with their splitting and smashing accompaniments were resumed.

Kemp stood in the passage trying to think. In a moment the Invisible Man would be in the kitchen. This door would not keep him a moment, and then...

A ringing came at the front door again. It would be the policemen. He ran into the hall, put up the chain and drew the bolts. He made the girl speak before he dropped the chain, and the three people blundered into the house in a heap, and Kemp slammed the door again.

"The Invisible Man!" said Kemp. "He has a revolver, with two shots – left. He's killed Adye. Shot him anyhow. Didn't you see him on the lawn? He's lying there."

"Who?" said one of the policemen.

"Adye," said Kemp.

"We came round the back way," said the girl.

"What's that smashing?" asked one of the policemen.

"He's in the kitchen – or will be. He has found an axe..."

Suddenly the house was full of the Invisible Man's resounding blows on the kitchen door. The girl stared towards the kitchen, shuddered and retreated into the dining room. Kemp tried to explain in broken sentences. They heard the kitchen door give.

"This way," cried Kemp, starting into activity, and bundled the policemen into the dining-room doorway.

"Poker," said Kemp, and rushed to the fender. He handed a poker to each policeman. He suddenly flung himself backwards.

"Whup!" said one policeman, ducked and caught the axe on his poker. The pistol snapped its penultimate shot and ripped a valuable Sidney Cooper.* The second policeman brought his poker down on the little weapon, as one might knock down a wasp, and sent it rattling to the floor.

At the first clash the girl screamed, stood screaming for a moment by the fireplace, and then ran to open the shutters – possibly with an idea of escaping by the shattered window.

The axe receded into the passage, and fell to a position about two feet from the ground. They could hear the Invisible Man breathing. "Stand away, you two," he said. "I want that man Kemp."

"We want you," said the first policeman, making a quick step forward and wiping with his poker at the Voice. The Invisible Man must have started back. He blundered into the umbrella stand. Then, as the policeman staggered with the swing of the blow he had aimed, the Invisible Man countered with the axe, the helmet crumpled like paper, and the blow sent the man spinning to the floor at the head of the kitchen stairs. But the second policeman, aiming behind the axe with his poker, hit something soft that snapped. There was a sharp exclamation of pain and the axe fell to the ground. The policeman wiped again at vacancy and hit nothing; he put his foot on the axe and struck again. Then he stood, poker clubbed, listening intent for the slightest movement.

He heard the dining-room window open and a quick rush of feet within. His companion rolled over and sat up, with the blood running down between his eye and ear. "Where is he?" asked the man on the floor.

"Don't know. I've hit him. He's standing somewhere in the hall. Unless he's slipped past you. Dr Kemp – sir."

Pause.

"Dr Kemp," cried the policeman again.

The second policeman struggled to his feet. He stood up. Suddenly the faint pad of bare feet on the kitchen stairs could be heard. "Yap!" cried the first policeman, and incontinently flung his poker. It smashed a little gas bracket.

He made as if he would pursue the Invisible Man downstairs. Then he thought better of it and stepped into the dining room.

"Dr Kemp," he began, and stopped short—

"Dr Kemp's in here," he said, as his companion looked over his shoulder.

The dining-room window was wide open, and neither housemaid nor Kemp was to be seen.

The second policeman's opinion of Kemp was terse and vivid.

28

The Hunter Hunted

MR HEELAS, MR KEMP'S nearest neighbour among the villa holders, was asleep in his summer house when the siege of Kemp's house began. Mr Heelas was one of the sturdy minority who refused to believe "in all this nonsense" about an invisible man. His wife, however, as he was to be reminded subsequently, did. He insisted upon walking about his garden just as if nothing was the matter, and he went to sleep in the afternoon in accordance with the custom of years. He slept through the smashing of the windows, and then woke up suddenly with a curious persuasion of something wrong. He looked across at Kemp's house, rubbed his eyes and looked again. Then he put his feet to the ground and sat listening. He said he was damned, and still the strange thing was visible. The house looked as though it had been deserted for weeks – after a violent riot. Every window was broken, and every window, save those of the belvedere study, was blinded by the internal shutters.

"I could have sworn it was all right" – he looked at his watch – "twenty minutes ago."

He became aware of a measured concussion and the clash of glass, far away in the distance. And then, as he sat open-mouthed, came a still more wonderful thing. The shutters of the dining-room window were flung open violently, and the housemaid in her outdoor hat and garments, appeared struggling in a frantic manner to throw up the sash. Suddenly a man appeared beside her, helping her – Dr Kemp! In another moment the window was open, and the housemaid was struggling out; she pitched forward and vanished among the shrubs. Mr Heelas stood up, exclaiming vaguely and vehemently at all these wonderful things. He saw Kemp stand on the sill, spring from the window and reappear almost instantaneously running along a path in the shrubbery and stooping as he ran, like a man who evades observation. He vanished behind a laburnum, and appeared again clambering a fence that abutted on the open down. In a second he had tumbled over and was running at a tremendous pace down the slope towards Mr Heelas.

"Lord!" cried Mr Heelas, struck with an idea. "It's that Invisible Man brute! It's right, after all!"

With Mr Heelas to think things like that was to act, and his cook watching him from the top window was amazed to see him come pelting towards the house at a good nine miles an hour. "Thought he wasn't afraid," said the cook. "Mary, just come here!" There was a slamming of doors, a ringing of bells and the voice of Mr Heelas bellowing like a bull. "Shut the doors, shut the windows, shut everything! The Invisible Man is coming!" Instantly the house was full of screams and directions and scurrying feet. He ran to shut the French windows himself that opened on the veranda; as he did so Kemp's head and shoulders and knee appeared over the edge of the garden fence. In another moment Kemp had ploughed through the asparagus and was running across the tennis lawn to the house.

"You can't come in," said Mr Heelas, shutting the bolts. "I'm very sorry if he's after you, but you can't come in!"

Kemp appeared with a face of terror close to the glass, rapping and then shaking frantically at the French window. Then, seeing his efforts were useless, he ran along the veranda, vaulted the end and went to hammer at the side door. Then he ran round by the side gate to the front of the house, and so into the hill road. And Mr Heelas staring from his window – a face of horror – had scarcely witnessed Kemp vanish ere the asparagus was being trampled this way and that by feet unseen. At that Mr Heelas fled precipitately upstairs, and the rest of the chase is beyond his purview. But as he passed the staircase window, he heard the side gate slam.

Emerging into the hill road, Kemp naturally took the downward direction, and so it was he came to run in his own person the very race he had watched with such a critical eye from the belvedere study only four days ago. He ran it well for a man out of training, and though his face was white and wet, his wits were cool to the last. He ran with wide strides, and wherever a patch of rough ground intervened, wherever there came a patch of raw flints or a bit of broken glass shone dazzling, he crossed it and left the bare invisible feet that followed to take what line they would.

For the first time in his life, Kemp discovered that the hill road was indescribably vast and desolate, and that the beginnings of the town far below at the hill foot were strangely remote. Never had there been a slower or more painful method of progression than running. All the gaunt villas, sleeping in the afternoon sun, looked locked and barred; no doubt they were locked and barred – by his own orders. But at any rate they might have kept a lookout for an eventuality like this! The town was rising up now, the sea had dropped out of sight behind it, and people down below were stirring. A tram was just arriving at the hill foot. Beyond that was the police station. Was that footsteps he heard behind him? Spurt.

The people below were staring at him, one or two were running, and his breath was beginning to saw in his throat. The tram was quite near now, and the Jolly Cricketers was noisily barring its doors. Beyond the tram were posts and heaps of gravel – the drainage works. He had a transitory idea of jumping into the tram and slamming the doors, and then he resolved to go for the police station. In another moment he had passed the door of the Jolly Cricketers, and was in the blistering fag end of the street, with human beings about him. The tram driver and his helper – arrested by the sight of his furious haste – stood staring with the tram horses unhitched. Further on the astonished features of navvies* appeared above the mounds of gravel.

His pace broke a little, and then he heard the swift pad of his pursuer and leapt forward again. "The Invisible Man!" he cried to the navvies, with a vague indicative gesture, and by an inspiration leapt the excavation and placed a burly group between him and the chase. Then, abandoning the idea of the police station, he turned into a little side street, rushed by a greengrocer's cart, hesitated for the tenth of a second at the door of a sweetstuff shop and then made for the mouth of an alley that ran back into the main Hill Street again. Two or three little children were playing here, and shrieked and scattered running at his apparition, and forthwith doors and windows opened and excited mothers revealed their hearts. Out he shot into Hill Street again, three hundred yards from the tramline end, and immediately he became aware of a tumultuous vociferation and running people.

He glanced up the street towards the hill. Hardly a dozen yards off ran a huge navvy, cursing in fragments and slashing viciously with a spade, and hard behind him came the tram conductor with his fists clenched. Up the street others followed these two, striking and shouting. Down towards the town, men and women were running, and he noticed clearly one man coming out of a shop door with a stick in his hand. "Spread out! Spread out!" cried someone. Kemp suddenly grasped the altered condition of the chase. He stopped and looked round, panting. "He's close here!" he cried. "Form a line across—"

"Aha!" shouted a voice.

He was hit hard under the ear, and went reeling, trying to face round towards his unseen antagonist. He just managed to keep his feet, and he struck a vain counter in the air. Then he was hit again under the jaw, and sprawled headlong on the ground. In another moment a knee compressed his diaphragm, and a couple of eager hands gripped his throat, but the grip of one was weaker than the other; he grasped the wrists, heard a cry of pain from his assailant, and then the spade of the navvy came whirling through the air above him and struck something with a dull thud. He felt a drop of moisture on his face. The grip at his throat suddenly relaxed, and with a convulsive effort Kemp loosed himself, grasped a limp shoulder and rolled uppermost. He gripped the unseen elbows near the ground. "I've got him!" screamed Kemp. "Help! Help hold! He's down! Hold his feet!"

In another second there was a simultaneous rush upon the struggle, and a stranger coming into the road suddenly might have thought an exceptionally savage game of rugby football was in progress. And there was no shouting after Kemp's cry – only a sound of blows and feet and a heavy breathing.

Then came a mighty effort, and the Invisible Man threw off a couple of his antagonists and rose to his knees. Kemp clung to him in front like a hound to a stag, and a dozen hands gripped, clutched and tore at the Unseen. The tram conductor suddenly got the neck and shoulders and lugged him back.

Down went the heap of struggling men again and rolled over. There was, I am afraid, some savage kicking. Then suddenly a wild scream of "Mercy! Mercy!" that died down swiftly to a sound like choking.

"Get back, you fools!" cried the muffled voice of Kemp, and there was a vigorous shoving-back of stalwart forms. "He's hurt, I tell you. Stand back!"

There was a brief struggle to clear a space, and then the circle of eager eyes saw the doctor kneeling, as it seemed, fifteen inches in the air, and holding invisible arms to the ground. Behind him a constable gripped invisible ankles.

"Don't you leave go of en," cried the big navvy, holding a bloodstained spade. "He's shamming."

"He's not shamming," said the doctor, cautiously raising his knee, "and I'll hold him." His face was bruised and already going red; he spoke thickly because of a bleeding lip. He released one hand and seemed to be feeling at the face. "The mouth's all wet," he said. And then, "Good God!"

He stood up abruptly and then knelt down on the ground by the side of the thing unseen. There was a pushing and shuffling, a sound of heavy feet as fresh people turned up to increase the pressure of the crowd. People now were coming out of the houses. The doors of the Jolly Cricketers were suddenly wide open. Very little was said.

Kemp felt about, his hand seeming to pass through empty air. "He's not breathing," he said, and then. "I can't feel his heart. His side – ugh!"

Suddenly an old woman, peering under the arm of the big navvy, screamed sharply. "Looky there!" she said, and thrust out a wrinkled finger.

And looking where she pointed, everyone saw, faint and transparent as though it was made of glass, so that veins and arteries and bones and nerves could be distinguished, the outline of a hand, a hand limp and prone. It grew clouded and opaque even as they stared.

"Hullo!" cried the constable. "Here's his feet a-showing!"

And so, slowly, beginning at his hands and feet and creeping along his limbs to the vital centres of his body, that strange change continued. It was like the slow spreading of a poison. First came the little white nerves, a hazy grey sketch of a limb, then the glassy bones and intricate arteries, then the flesh and skin, first a faint fogginess and then growing rapidly dense and opaque. Presently they could see his crushed chest and his shoulders, and the dim outline of his drawn and battered features.

When at last the crowd made way for Kemp to stand erect, there lay, naked and pitiful on the ground, the bruised and broken body of a young man about thirty. His hair and beard were white – not grey with age but white with the whiteness of albinism, and his eyes were like garnets. His hands were clenched, his eyes wide open, and his expression was one of anger and dismay.

"Cover his face!" said a man. "For Gawd's sake, cover that face!" and three little children, pushing forward through the crowd, were suddenly twisted round and sent packing off again.

Someone brought a sheet from the Jolly Cricketers, and having covered him, they carried him into that house. And there, on a shabby bed in a tawdry, ill-lit bedroom, ended the strange experiment of the Invisible Man.

The Epilogue

S O ENDS THE STORY of the strange and evil experiment of the Invisible Man. And if you would learn more of him you must go to a little inn near Port Stowe and talk to the landlord. The sign of the inn is an empty board save for a hat and boots, and the name is the title of this story. The landlord is a short and corpulent little man with a nose of cylindrical protrusion, wiry hair and a sporadic rosiness of visage. Drink generously, and he will tell you generously of all the things that happened to him after that time, and of how the lawyers tried to do him out of the treasure found upon him.

"When they found they couldn't prove whose money was which, I'm blessed," he says, "if they didn't try to make me out a blooming treasure trove!* Do I *look* like a treasure trove? And then a gentleman gave me a guinea a night to tell the story at the Empire Music 'all – just tell 'em in my own words – barring one."

And if you want to cut off the flow of his reminiscences abruptly, you can always do so by asking if there weren't three manuscript books in the story. He admits there were and proceeds to explain, with asseverations that everybody thinks *he* has 'em! But bless you! he hasn't. "The Invisible Man it was took 'em off to hide 'em when I cut and ran for Port Stowe. It's that Mr Kemp put people on with the idea of *my* having 'em."

And then he subsides into a pensive state, watches you furtively, bustles nervously with glasses and presently leaves the bar.

He is a bachelor man – his tastes were ever bachelor, and there are no womenfolk in the house. Outwardly he buttons – it is expected of him – but in his more vital privacies, in the matter of braces for example, he still turns to string. He conducts his house without enterprise, but with eminent decorum. His movements are slow, and he is a great thinker. But he has a reputation for wisdom and for a respectable parsimony in the village, and his knowledge of the roads of the south of England would beat Cobbett.*

And on Sunday mornings, every Sunday morning all the year round, while he is closed to the outer world, and every night after ten, he goes into his bar parlour bearing a glass of gin faintly tinged with water; and having placed this down, he locks the door and examines the blinds, and even looks under the table. And then, being satisfied of his solitude, he unlocks the cupboard and a box in the cupboard and a drawer in that box, and produces three volumes bound in brown leather, and places them solemnly in the middle of the table. The covers are weather-worn and tinged with an algal green – for once they sojourned in a ditch, and some of the pages have been washed blank by dirty water. The landlord sits down in an armchair, fills a long clay pipe slowly – gloating over the books the while. Then he pulls one towards him and opens it, and begins to study it – turning over the leaves backwards and forwards.

His brows are knit and his lips move painfully. "Hex, little two up in the air, cross and a fiddle-de-dee. Lord! What a one he was for intellect!"

Presently he relaxes and leans back, and blinks through his smoke across the room at things invisible to other eyes. "Full of secrets," he says. "Wonderful secrets!

"Once I get the haul of them – *Lord!*

"I wouldn't do what *he* did: I'd just – well!" He pulls at his pipe.

So he lapses into a dream, the undying wonderful dream of his life. And though Kemp has fished unceasingly, and Adye has questioned closely, no human being save the landlord knows those books are there, with the subtle secret of invisibility and a dozen other strange secrets written therein. And none other will know of them until he dies.

Note on the Text

This edition is based on the 1924 Atlantic edition, but incorporates some readings from the second 1897 Pearson edition. The spelling and punctuation have been standardized, modernized and made consistent throughout.

Notes

p. 10, *clock-jobber*: A person who mends clocks.

p. 24, *National School*: "National" schools were church schools for the children of the poor founded in the nineteenth century by the National Society for Promoting Religious Education.

p. 24, *compared the stranger to the man with the one talent*: A reference to the Parable of the Talents in the Gospel of Matthew (25:14–30). In this story, a man leaves his money in the hands of his three servants, entrusting to them five talents, two talents and one talent respectively (a talent being a sum of money). The first two servants trade with the money they have been given and increase its value, and are consequently rewarded by their master on his return. The third, however, instead buries his one talent in the ground, therefore failing to increase its value, and is punished.

p. 25, *Whitsuntide*: The seventh Sunday after Easter, commemorating the descent of the Holy Spirit on the disciples of Jesus.

p. 28, *At staring... starts scratch*: In other words, Cuss, wearing nothing on his face, cannot match the other's implacable stare.

p. 38, *ordinary bicycles*: Another name for penny-farthings.

p. 38, *the Jubilee*: The Golden Jubilee of 1887, which celebrated the fiftieth anniversary of Queen Victoria's accession to the throne.

p. 41, *the result was Babel*: In the Book of Genesis (11:1–9) the builders of the Tower of Babel, who had attempted to make the structure so tall that it would reach heaven, are punished by God by being made to speak a multitude of mutually unintelligible languages.

p. 45, *Unitarian*: Unitarianism is a Protestant denomination that rejects the Holy Trinity, emphasizing the unity of God and the humanity of Christ, and in general is noted for the liberalism of its approach to dogma and theology.

p. 50, *peewit*: Another name for the lapwing.

p. 52, *Vox et – what is it? – jabber*: Marvel is thinking of the Latin phrase *vox et præterea nihil* ("a voice and nothing else"), from the *Moralia* by the Greek author Plutarch (*c*.AD 46–*c*.120).

p. 58, *subsequent proceedings interested him no more*: From the comic poem 'The Society upon the Stanislaus' by the American writer Francis Bret Harte (1839–1902): "Then Abner Dean of Angel's raised a point of order, when / A chunk of old red sandstone took him in the abdomen, / And he smiled a kind of sickly smile, and curled up on the floor, / And the subsequent proceedings interested him no more."

p. 60, *Tap*: The visitor is looking for the taproom, the area in a public house where drinks are available on tap.

p. 74, *Alteration*: The mariner means "altercation".

p. 79, *the Royal Society*: A prestigious scientific society founded by Charles II in 1660.

p. 80, *glairy*: Slimy and viscid, like an egg white.

p. 82, *Burton*: Beer brewed in Burton on Trent in Staffordshire.

p. 85, *I'm out of frocks*: The barman means that he is not a child. (At the time both little girls and little boys wore frocks.)

p. 85, *leveret*: A young hare.

p. 94, *pharynx and nares*: The pharynx is the cavity in the throat connecting the nose and mouth to the oesophagus. The nares are the nostrils.

p. 97, *nauplii and tornarias*: The larvae of, respectively, some species of crustacean and the acorn worm (a small, burrowing marine animal).

p. 99, *cum grano*: An abbreviation of the Latin phrase *cum grano salis* ("with a grain of salt").

p. 109, *Röntgen vibrations*: Griffin is describing X-rays, discovered by the German physicist Wilhelm Conrad Röntgen (1845–1923) in 1895.

p. 109, *Tapetum*: A reflective layer of tissue on the eyes of some animals, including cats, which makes them shine in the dark.

p. 112, *strychnine... the Palaeolithic in a bottle*: Strychnine, a highly poisonous substance obtained from the nux vomica tree, was occasionally used in the late nineteenth and early twentieth centuries as a stimulant. As a scientist, Kemp regards this practice as outdated (hence "Palaeolithic").

p. 113, *German silver*: A copper alloy with nickel and zinc.

p. 119, *hansom*: A two-wheeled horse-drawn carriage.

p. 120, *Mudie's*: Mudie's Lending Library, founded by Charles Edward Mudie (1818–90) and based on New Oxford Street in London.

p. 120, *the Museum*: The British Museum.

p. 121, '*When Shall We See His Face?*': Many hymns contain similar lines, such as 'Come, We That Love the Lord' by the English hymn writer and poet Isaac Watts (1674–1748): "There shall we see His face, / And never, never sin; / There, from the rivers of His grace, / Drink endless pleasures in."

p. 122, *Crusoe's solitary discovery*: A reference to the shipwrecked Robinson Crusoe's discovery of a footprint on the island that he had thought deserted, in the novel by the English novelist and journalist Daniel Defoe (1660–1731).

p. 128, '*Dust to dust, earth to earth*': From the burial service in the Book of Common Prayer, the official service book of the Church of England, first issued in 1549: "Earth to earth, ashes to ashes, dust to dust."

p. 129, *a view hallo*: A cry uttered by a huntsman when a fox breaks cover.

p. 132, *dominoes*: A domino was a cloak-and-mask combination worn at masquerades.

p. 132, *a cheval glass*: A large mirror.

p. 136, *Louis Quatorze vest*: That is, a waistcoat in a style associated with the reign of the French king Louis XIV (1638–1715), who reigned 1643–1715.

p. 137, *benzoline*: A stain-remover.

p. 140, *Delilah*: In the Old Testament, Delilah betrays Samson to the Philistines by revealing that his strength is in his long hair (Judges 16).

p. 144, *Reign of Terror*: The term used to refer to the period of the French Revolution from September 1793 to July 1794, which was characterized by bloody violence and mass executions.

p. 156, *contra mundum*: "Against the world" (Latin).

p. 163, *Sidney Cooper*: Thomas Sidney Cooper (1803–1902), an English landscape painter.

p. 169, *navvies*: Labourers involved in road, railway or canal construction.

p. 173, *try to make me out a blooming treasure trove*: Until 1996, under British law any valuables discovered buried underground or otherwise hidden and of unknown ownership became the property of the Crown.

p. 174, *Cobbett*: The English writer William Cobbett (1763–1835), author of *Rural Rides* (1830), an account of a series of journeys by horseback through the southern English countryside.

Extra Material

on

H.G. Wells's

The Invisible Man

H.G. Wells's Life

Herbert George Wells, known as "Bertie" at home, was born on 21st September 1866 at Atlas House, a shop on the high street in Bromley, Kent, where his family lived and where his father, Joseph (Joe) Wells, sold china and cricket accessories. Joe, a somewhat feckless and irresponsible character, was in perpetual financial difficulties, and only managed to make ends meet with what he earned in his second job as a professional cricketer and cricket coach. As a child Bertie attended the Bromley Academy, where he excelled, learning skills necessary for trade, such as bookkeeping and copperplate handwriting, but Joe struggled to pay his son's school fees, a problem exacerbated in 1877 when he fell from a ladder and broke his leg, cutting short his sporting career. As a result, the family's economic situation deteriorated, and in 1880, when Bertie was thirteen, his mother, Sarah (née Neal), accepted the post of housekeeper at Uppark, the country house on the South Downs near Midhurst in West Sussex where she had worked before her marriage. Intent on her sons' social advancement, she also decided that the time had come for Bertie to follow his two elder brothers into the drapery trade, and so abruptly ended his education.

First Years in Bromley

Wells's first experience as a draper's apprentice – in Windsor – lasted no longer than his probationary month, as he proved unable (or unwilling) to apply the skills he had learnt at the Bromley Academy in practice. This was followed by a second false start when a plan for him to become a pupil teacher (a senior pupil who also teaches younger students) at a new school in Wookey, Somerset, fell through, after which he had no choice but to go to stay with his mother in the servants' quarters at Uppark. His next employment was as an apprentice in a chemist's shop at Church Hill, Midhurst. During this time Wells took lessons in Latin (necessary for his pharmaceutical work) with Horace Byatt, the headmaster of Midhurst Grammar School, with whom he briefly lived as a boarding pupil after his trial month at the chemist's had ended – his family's finances

Apprenticeships and the Normal School

again making it impossible for him to continue with his training. This agreeable and profitable interlude was curtailed when his mother arranged for him to take on an apprenticeship at Hyde's Drapery Emporium in Southsea. He was profoundly unhappy in this situation, but found an escape after two years when, having pleaded with Byatt, he was offered a post as a pupil teacher at Midhurst. His academic progress was swift, and a year later, in 1884, he went to the Normal School (later the Royal College) of Science in South Kensington, west London, where he studied biology for a year under "Darwin's bulldog", Thomas Henry Huxley. The next year he studied physics, and the year after that geology, but as time went on he neglected his studies in favour of politics – he had become a keen socialist, preaching at the student debating society and attending William Morris's meetings at Hammersmith. During this period, he founded the *Science Schools Journal*, in which his first writings appeared, notably 'The Chronic Argonauts', a precursor to *The Time Machine*. Partly as a result of these distractions, in 1887 he failed his final examination, leaving the university without a degree.

In August of the same year, Wells, then twenty-one, took a job as a teacher at Holt Academy, a boarding school in North Wales, but was soon forced to resign due to ill health, having injured his kidneys and lungs during a game of football and becoming consumptive as a result. After a period of convalescence at Uppark, in autumn 1888 he embarked on a new teaching job, at Henley House School in Kilburn, north London, where his pupils included A.A. Milne. Soon afterwards he was offered a position as tutor in a correspondence college for students at London University that had been set up by a man named William Briggs, and it was while in this, more comfortable role that, in 1890, Wells finally gained his BSc in zoology from the university – with first-class honours.

Marriages to Isabel and Jane

On 30th October 1891 Wells married his cousin Isabel Mary Wells, at whose home he had lodged during his time in London, and thereafter the couple set up house at 28 Haldon Road, Wandsworth. The marriage, however, was not successful, since Wells was unable to adapt to the life of staid domesticity that Isabel wanted. The decisive factor in the failure of the union, though, was sexual incompatibility: Wells later wrote that for Isabel "lovemaking was nothing more than an outrage inflicted upon reluctant womankind". The young teacher very soon fell in love with one of his students, Amy Catherine Robbins, known to Wells as Jane, who was six years his junior and whom he regarded as possessing the intellectual curiosity that his cousin lacked. The pair eloped, marrying on 27th October 1895 (following Wells's divorce from Isabel), having cohabited from January 1894 in lodgings at Mornington Place, Camden Town. The remainder of the decade saw moves to Sevenoaks in Kent and Woking and Worcester Park in Surrey. Although Wells found his second marriage no more sexually satisfying than his first, it survived, producing two sons: George Philip (Gip), born in 1901, who became a zoologist, and Frank Richard, born in 1903, who went on to work in the film industry.

During the early 1890s, while working as a tutor in biology, Wells began to supplement his income from teaching by writing: as well as penning his *Textbook of Biology* (1893), he edited the magazine of Briggs's college, the *University Correspondent*, and wrote for the *Educational Times*. In 1893 a recurrence of tuberculosis forced him to give up teaching altogether, and from then onwards he attempted to support himself entirely on his literary output. He determined that to achieve recognition he should produce more work in the vein of 'The Chronic Argonauts', and began to write fiction and reviews for the *Saturday Review* and *Pall Mall Gazette*. Encouraged by the poet W.E. Henley, editor of the *New Review*, Wells reworked the material in the earlier story, and in 1895 *The Time Machine* was published, to great acclaim, in the January to May numbers of Henley's periodical, with book versions becoming available on both sides of the Atlantic in June of the same year. That Wells's star was in the ascendant in this period was reflected in the steep increase in his earnings, which doubled over two years: from £381 in 1893 to £792 in 1895. More books quickly appeared, many of them further "scientific romances", including *The Island of Doctor Moreau* (1896), *The Invisible Man* (1897), *The War of the Worlds* (1898), *When the Sleeper Wakes* (1899) and *The First Men in the Moon* (1901).

After a further attack of ill health in 1898, Wells was advised to move away from the city, and as a result commissioned the architect C.F.A. Voysey to design a home on the cliffs overlooking the English Channel in Sandgate in Kent, which would be suitable for him in the event of his requiring a wheelchair. At this new abode, Spade House, completed in 1900, he rubbed shoulders with the likes of Joseph Conrad, Ford Madox Ford and Henry James, all of whom lived nearby, and entertained many others, including the novelists Arnold Bennett and George Gissing.

By the early twentieth century, Wells was established as a successful author of popular fiction. But, anxious not to be remembered only as the English Jules Verne, he endeavoured to vary his work and produce the kind of literature that would put him on a par with great writers of the day. To this end, in 1900 he wrote *Love and Mr Lewisham*, a semi-autobiographical comic

The Time Machine and Early Success

Comic Realism and Prophetic Writings

novel about a young teacher that eschewed fantastical elements in favour of realism. Further works in this mode followed, all of which were set in the English Home Counties and featured characters who, like the author, were of a lower-middle-class social background: a draper's apprentice in the case of the eponymous hero of *Kipps* (1905); a shopkeeper in the case of *The History of Mr Polly* (1910). Another, more ambitious realist novel of the Edwardian period, *Tono-Bungay* (1909) – whose young protagonist experiences an "extensive cross-section of the British social organism" – was an early-twentieth-century version of the panoramic satires, or "condition of England" novels, of the High Victorians.

Wells also regarded himself as a social prophet, and this found expression during the early years of the new century in a number of works of both fiction and non-fiction. His first attempt was *Anticipations* (1902), a collection of essays warning of the dangers to humanity of scientific and technological development and arguing for the abolition of existing structures of social organization, such as monarchies and nation states, and their replacement with a "new republic". This socialist outlook was further expounded in *A Modern Utopia* (1905), a traveller's account of a planet identical to the Earth, but whose denizens inhabit an ideal world state organized according to socialist principles and ruled by a meritocracy of "voluntary noblemen" known as the Samurai.

Clash with the Fabian Society

The views expressed in *Anticipations* led to an invitation in 1903 to join the Fabian Society, an organization founded at the turn of the century to campaign for a gradual, rather than revolutionary, transition to socialism. This brought Wells into contact with its leaders, known as the "Old Gang", notably Sidney and Beatrice Webb and the Irish playwright George Bernard Shaw. However, Wells proved a less than compliant member, delivering in February 1906 a paper titled 'The Faults of the Fabian', in which he lambasted the organization for its sluggishness and genteel complacency and argued for greater radicalism and a vast expansion in membership. Wells was in effect attempting to take control of the society, which responded by setting up a committee to review its organization, finances and activities, to be headed by Wells. Ultimately, however, its proposals were not accepted, leading to Wells's resignation from the society in 1908. He wrote later: "No part of my career rankles so acutely in my memory with the conviction of bad judgement... as that storm in the Fabian teacup."

The Old Gang had also objected to Wells's views on sexual morality. Wells was a believer in polygamy, or free love, something that he expressed in the 1906 novel *In the Days of the*

Comet, in which the central character pursues a *ménage à quatre* involving his wife and another couple. For Wells, a conventional socialist belief in emancipation from economic exploitation went hand in hand with a desire for emancipation from the sexual exploitation represented by marriage. He failed, however, to persuade his fellow Fabians to share his views, and the novel was widely criticized.

Indeed, despite the longevity of his second marriage, Wells was deeply frustrated and repeatedly sought sexual fulfilment elsewhere – just as he had previously when he left Isabel for Jane – later recording the details in a third volume of autobiography, which was published posthumously in 1984 as *H.G. Wells in Love* (the two volumes of his *Experiment in Autobiography* having appeared in 1934). Furthermore, Jane was aware of and even tolerated the serial infidelities of her husband. His many "*passades*" (as he called them) included affairs with the writers Dorothy Richardson, Elizabeth von Arnim and Violet Hunt.

Extramarital Affairs and Amber Reeves

Among the extramarital dalliances indulged in by Wells, who described himself as a "Don Juan among the intelligentsia", were relationships with two members of the "Fabian Nursery" group of eager young socialists. The first was Rosamund Bland, the daughter of one of the founders of the Fabian Society, Hubert Bland (and the adopted daughter of Bland's wife, the writer Edith Nesbit). The second, and more significant, one was a twenty-one-year-old Cambridge graduate, Amber Reeves, who was a frequent guest at Spade House and became Wells's protégée. When Amber fell pregnant in April 1909, the couple eloped to Le Touquet in France, but this proved unsuccessful, as Wells found himself unwilling to sever his links with his old life. They returned to England, where Reeves – at her own suggestion – married a man named Rivers Blanco-White, who had proposed to her previously and was fully aware of her situation. The daughter born of the affair, Anna-Jane, was raised as Blanco-White's child. Reeves's relationship with Wells, however, became the subject of gossip within the Fabian circle, and a scandal arose, which threatened Wells's standing as a respected public figure. The novel *Ann Veronica* (1909), an escapist fantasy about a middle-aged teacher who elopes with one of his students, was a thinly veiled fictionalization of the entanglement.

Partly as a consequence of this episode, the Wellses moved back to London, to 17 Church Row, Hampstead; but being so close to the epicentre of metropolitan gossip made Wells uncomfortable, and so in 1911 he rented the Old Rectory, later renamed Easton Glebe, a secluded Georgian house on the Easton estate in Essex, owned by the eccentric and bohemian Lady

Easton Glebe, Quarrel with Henry James and Meeting with Rebecca West

Warwick. The frenetic weekend house parties held by the Wellses at the Glebe in the ensuing years, which were attended by the great and the good of the day and characterized by boisterous hockey matches and other games, became an institution, and were described by one guest, the writer Frank Swinnerton, as "whirls of unceasing activity".

During the period following the move to Easton Glebe, Wells quarrelled with his friend and long-term correspondent Henry James. The dispute concerned the two writers' differing conceptions of the novel: for James it was a work of art; for Wells it was "the only medium through which we can discuss the great majority of the problems which are being raised in such bristling multitude by our contemporary social development", as he described it in a lecture of May 1911. Ultimately, as Wells told James, he would rather be a journalist than an artist. The disagreement came to a head with the publication of *Boon* (1915), in which Wells included a cruel caricature of James and satirical pastiches of his style. This deeply wounded James, who considered the book "bad manners", and brought their friendship to an end.

It was also at Easton Glebe that Wells began another of his long-term affairs, this time with the writer Rebecca West, later famous as the author of *Black Lamb and Grey Falcon* (1941) and for her coverage of the Nuremberg trials. The pair met because of a scathing review by the suffragist and radical West, who was then nineteen, of Wells's novel *Marriage* (1912) – about an unhappily married couple who banish themselves to the wilderness of Labrador and thereby succeed in saving their relationship – in the feminist journal *The Freewoman*, which caught his attention. He invited her to his home to discuss it, a meeting that sparked an attachment that would last for a decade and produce a son, Anthony West, who was born on the day of Britain's declaration of war against Germany, 4th August 1914.

First World War and the League of Nations

The First World War had in many ways been predicted in Wells's fiction, notably in 'The Land Ironclads' (1903), a short story that foresaw the invention of the tank, *The War in the Air* (1908), which envisaged the use of aircraft in warfare, and *The World Set Free* (1914), which described a devastating world war, in the aftermath of which mankind reorganizes itself in the form of an enlightened world state. Wells, at forty-eight too old to join the fighting, nevertheless argued strongly – in *The War That Will End War* (1914) – in favour of the war against Germany, and in somewhat chauvinistic terms, something he later regretted when it became clear that the conflict was unlikely to bring about the unification of mankind that he desired. He provided a fictionalized account of his journey from hysterical bellicosity to disillusionment and despair in the novel *Mr Britling Sees It Through* (1916), which was reprinted twelve times before the end of the year of its publication, making it one of the most popular books of the war. In 1917 he campaigned for the creation of a "League of Free Nations", and in 1918 was invited by Lord Northcliffe, the minister for propaganda, to chair the British government's Committee for Propaganda in Enemy Country, an experience that Wells, who sought to use this position to advance his ideas about the League of Nations and the need for great social change, found deeply frustrating when he realized that the victorious powers were not interested in weakening their commitment to the principle of strong nation states.

Disappointed by this experience, after the war Wells decided that he would be better off using his writing to communicate his ideas, and produced an educational textbook, *The Outline of History* (1920), an ambitious work that provided a chronicle of human civilization slanted to reflect his own world view. More textbooks followed: *A Short History of the World* (1922), *The Science of Life* (1930) – on which he collaborated with his son Gip and Julian Huxley, grandson of T.H. – and *The Work, Wealth and Happiness of Mankind* (1931).

In September 1920, at the invitation of his friend Maxim Gorky, Wells visited Russia, where he met Lenin, later describing the encounter as "a very uphill argument". Trotsky wrote that the Communist leader had later said of Wells, "Ugh! What a narrow petty bourgeois he is! He is a philistine!" – a remark which Anthony West claims, in his biography of his father, was a fabrication. Although the trip was criticized by Winston Churchill, who was concerned that Wells might use his considerable influence to promote sympathy for the Bolsheviks, it contributed to a healing of the rift between Wells and the Left in Britain that had been caused by his jingoism during the early part of the war, and in November 1921 Wells was invited to stand as the Labour candidate for the London University seat in the general election of the following year. He failed to win (in fact he came last), but stood again the following year when the Conservative government fell, although this too was unsuccessful.

Visit to Russia

By 1923 Rebecca West, now a writer with a growing reputation, had come to realize that Wells would never leave Jane, and so ended their relationship. Shortly afterwards, Wells, on a trip to Geneva to see the League of Nations first-hand (an experience he found profoundly dispiriting), met a young Dutch author named Odette Keun, with whom he had been corresponding since he wrote a positive review of one of her books, and the two began an affair. Thereafter he spent much of his time with

Odette Keun and Death of Jane

Odette near the town of Grasse in the south of France, where he had a house built for the two of them, which he called "Lou Pidou" (an abbreviation of "Le Petit Dieu", Odette's pet name for Wells).

In May 1927 Jane discovered that she was suffering from an advanced form of cancer, and Wells returned to Easton Glebe from France to spend what time remained with his wife. She died on 6th October 1927. Despite his bereavement, Wells's literary output continued unabated, both fiction – such as *Mr Blettsworthy on Rampole Island* (1928) – and non-fiction, such as *The Open Conspiracy* (1928), another iteration of the author's belief in the need for a "new human community" led by a world government. Two years after Jane's death, Wells gave up Easton Glebe and moved back to London, living in a flat at 47 Chiltern Court, off Baker Street. He spent less and less time with Odette, and instead took up with the Russian adventuress and (double) agent Marie von Benckendorff, now Baroness Budberg, known as Moura, whom he had met at Gorky's house in Moscow in 1920 and with whom he had kept up a correspondence. Wells left Lou Pidou for the last time in May 1932.

With the world descending into crisis due to the spread of fascism and communism, in 1933 Wells wrote *The Shape of Things to Come*, a science-fiction work purporting to be written by a senior diplomat who has had visions of a historical textbook written in the far future that describes world events from the First World War to the year 2106. In it Wells predicted a world war (beginning in 1939) that would destroy civilization and result in the formation of a benign – albeit "Puritan" – tyranny, which in turn would pave the way for a utopian future. Then, in the spring and summer of 1934, he made, in quick succession, a visit to the United States to meet Franklin D. Roosevelt, whom Wells considered to be working towards the new world order that he had for so long advocated, and a further visit to the Soviet Union, this time to meet Stalin. The Soviet leader impressed Wells personally, but he was "acutely frustrated and disappointed" by his experience of Russia, and especially by the attempts being made there to suppress literary freedom. Significantly, shortly before this trip, Wells had succeeded John Galsworthy as president of PEN International, the organization set up in 1921 to promote contacts and cooperation between writers across the globe.

Declining Influence and Late Campaigns

In the same year, Wells published the two volumes of his *Experiment in Autobiography*, to generally favourable reviews, relocated to 13 Hanover Terrace, a grand Regency house overlooking Regent's Park, where he would remain for the rest of his life, and collaborated with the Hungarian filmmaker Alexander

Korda on an ambitious cinematic adaptation of *The Shape of Things to Come*, titled *Things to Come*, which was released two years later, in 1936. But as the decade went on, Wells's influence declined, and although books continued to appear – such as *The Anatomy of Frustration* and *The Croquet Player* in 1936 – the critical response was often that his writing was becoming repetitious and even careless. Wells came to be seen as old-fashioned, and finding publishers for his books became more difficult than it once was. In 1938 he told a correspondent: "I am tired, I am old, I am ill... My epitaph will be 'He was clever, but not clever enough'."

With characteristic prescience, from 1936 Wells devoted much of his energies to the concept of a "world encyclopedia". This he envisaged as a fusion of his existing educational books (such as *The Outline of History*) with other reference works to create a definitive pool of human knowledge, which would "hold men's minds together in... a common interpretation of reality" and thereby counter the influence of any of "the current *isms*". Unfortunately, progress on the idea was slow, and Wells had difficulty convincing a publisher to back it. *World Brain*, a collection of essays outlining Wells's thinking on the subject, was published in 1938.

In October 1939, shortly after the outbreak of the Second World War, Wells declared in a letter to *The Times* that he had written a statement of the rights of man – including the rights to welfare, education, free movement and so on – and subsequently formed a committee to create a more formal draft, which was published as *The Rights of Man* (1940). The campaign replaced the one for the world encyclopedia, and ultimately contributed to the Universal Declaration of Human Rights adopted by the United Nations in 1948.

Nevertheless, as the war progressed, Wells's standing and influence continued to decline. His health deteriorating, he spent more time at Hanover Terrace, involving himself in increasingly vexatious quarrels with rival writers and thinkers, including George Orwell, and continuing to churn out a barrage of polemical articles for the press, many of which were critical of the Catholic Church. In 1942–43 he completed a doctoral thesis in zoology for London University, hoping that it might help him to achieve his coveted goal of being made a Fellow of the Royal Society. It did not, something that was a cruel disappointment.

Final Years and Death

Wells published his last book in 1944, a brief, apocalyptic pamphlet called *Mind at the End of Its Tether*, which described in pessimistic terms the impending end of life on earth, the only glimmer of hope being that man might give way to some new animal that will become "the next Lord of Creation".

H.G. Wells died in his sleep at his home at Hanover Terrace on 13th August 1946, aged seventy-nine, and was cremated at Golders Green three days later. In a short speech during the ceremony, the writer J.B. Priestley described him as "the great prophet of our time".

H.G. Wells's Works

H.G. Wells was an enormously prolific writer, producing scores of books over more than sixty years in a variety of genres. What follows are descriptions of his better-known and more significant works.

The Time Machine   *The Time Machine*, published in 1895, was Wells's first full-length "scientific romance" and the book that made his name. It was a development of ideas he had explored in an earlier story, 'The Chronic Argonauts', which appeared in the *Science Schools Journal* in 1888. The new version was initially serialized in the January to May editions of the *New Review*, whose editor, W.E. Henley, had encouraged Wells to extend and rework the original tale. *The Time Machine* quickly came out in book form, published by Heinemann in London and Henry Holt & Co. in New York. The plot concerns a man, known throughout as "the Time Traveller", who, having invented a machine capable of travelling through time, journeys to the year 802,701, there discovering that the human race has diverged into two separate species – the beautiful but defenceless Eloi and the subterranean and degenerate Morlocks – who have evolved from, respectively, the leisured and proletarian classes of his own day. The novel established Wells as a pioneer of science fiction, and was a huge best-seller.

The Island of Dr Moreau   Wells lost no time in building on the success of *The Time Machine*, producing a number of works, many of them further "scientific romances", in a very short period. One such was *The Island of Dr Moreau* (1896), an adventure story narrated by Edward Prendick, who is shipwrecked and rescued by a passing boat carrying a cargo of wild animals destined for the island home of Dr Moreau, who is conducting experiments on animals in order to create half-human hybrids. The book proved controversial for its sensationalism, and was labelled indecent and even blasphemous by critics.

The Invisible Man   Next to appear was *The Invisible Man* (1897), like *The Island of Dr Moreau* a novella about the dangers of scientific advancement. It was originally serialized in *Pearson's Weekly* in 1897 and appeared in book form the following year. A mysterious stranger, his face obscured by bandages except for a fake nose, arrives at the local inn of a Sussex village, demanding that he be left alone and spending all of his time apparently conducting chemical experiments. During an altercation at the inn, the stranger reveals that he is in fact invisible, before fleeing. The man, whose name is Griffin, a scientist, seeks out an old colleague, Dr Kemp, to whom he explains his discovery of a method of changing a body's refractive index so that it neither absorbs nor reflects light and is thus rendered invisible. Griffin, apparently mad, describes his plan to exploit his discovery in order to create a "Reign of Terror" over the nation. However, he is betrayed by Kemp and later killed by a mob, his body once more becoming visible as he dies.

Like *The Invisible Man*, *The War of the Worlds* was serialized in *Pearson's Weekly* in 1897 before appearing in hardcover in 1898, published by Heinemann. The first part of the novel describes the invasion of southern England by hostile beings from Mars, beginning with a meteor that lands on Horsell Common in Surrey, quickly releasing tentacled aliens who use a heat ray to exterminate all the onlookers. With London devastated and the invasion complete, the second part describes the aftermath of the catastrophe, with the survivors living in hiding. The invasion is ultimately unsuccessful, however, due to the Martians' susceptibility to earthly bacteria. In common with many of Wells's science-fiction stories, *The War of the Worlds* has been adapted numerous times, perhaps the most famous version being the notorious radio broadcast by Orson Welles of 30th October 1938 on the CBS network in the United States, which used the conceit of live emergency news bulletins describing the arrival of Martians in New Jersey. Thousands of listeners were terrified, convinced that what they were hearing was real; H.G. Wells was reportedly furious.

The War of the Worlds

By the end of the nineteenth century, Wells, now enjoying considerable prosperity and acclaim, began to tire of his scientific romances, wishing to turn his hand to fiction in a more realistic mode. *Love and Mr Lewisham* (1900) was the first result of this transition, as well as the first of many novels to be based on the author's real-life experiences, containing a fictionalized account of his journey from Midhurst Grammar School to the Normal School in South Kensington. The story concerns Mr Lewisham, an impoverished eighteen-year-old teacher at a boys' school in Sussex, who falls in love with a young woman named Ethel Henderson. Later, when he is a student in London, and now a committed socialist, he meets Ethel again at a seance, and endeavours to free her from her spiritualist stepfather, who is a fraud. The book was well received, although some critics noted, in the words of one, "a disproportionate realism that almost amounted to vulgarity".

Love and Mr Lewisham

After returning briefly to the fantastical strand of his output with the next book, *The First Men in the Moon* (1901), Wells sought to establish himself as a political prophet, and published a series of articles in the *Fortnightly Review* in 1901 that later in the same year

Anticipations

appeared together under the title *Anticipations of the Reaction of Mechanical and Scientific Progress upon Human Life and Thought*, published by Macmillan. Wells subsequently described the book as "the keystone to the main arch of my work". As well as making predictions about developments in science and engineering, notably an explosion in motorized transportation leading to the dramatic expansion of suburbs, Wells foresaw the failure of democracy and a devastating war, resulting in the formation of a single world state, a "new republic" led by a scientific elite – ideas that would recur throughout his oeuvre. *Anticipations* was both a best-seller and a critical success – although modern readers may baulk at Wells's apparent advocacy of a form of eugenics – considerably increasing the author's standing as a public figure and influence as a thinker, and opening many doors, not least in bringing him into contact with the "Old Gang" of the socialist Fabian Society.

A Modern Utopia

Buoyed by the success of *Anticipations*, Wells produced more books in the futurological mode, one of the most significant being *A Modern Utopia* (1905), which, like *Anticipations*, was serialized in the *Fortnightly Review* before appearing almost immediately in book form. Influenced by More's *Utopia*, it has a "shot-silk texture" combining "imaginative narrative" and "philosophical discussion", as Wells described it in his preface. It concerns two characters, the narrator and his companion, who are transported from a walking tour of the Swiss Alps to a planet that is a duplicate of the Earth, but whose culture and political organization are radically different from those of Wells's Edwardian world. As in *Anticipations*, Wells envisaged an ideal global state ruled by an elite, this time described as a class of "voluntary noblemen" known as the Samurai, who preside over a world of "sane order". The book was received well by critics.

Kipps

In parallel to the strand of social prophecy exemplified by *A Modern Utopia*, Wells continued to produce realist fiction in the style of *Love and Mr Lewisham*. Like that book, *Kipps*, published by Macmillan in 1905, was semi-autobiographical, this time drawing on the author's experience as a tradesman's apprentice, largely for comic effect. It was one of several novels portraying the plight of lower-middle-class "little men" from southern England, people who, in the words of one character, are stuck "in a blessed drainpipe", doomed to crawl along it until they die. The eponymous Kipps, an orphaned and penniless draper's apprentice, is granted a means of escape, however, in the form of an unexpected legacy from a wealthy relative, and the later sections of the novel describe his clumsy attempts to adapt to his elevated social station. *Kipps* was not an instant commercial success, but Henry James considered it a "masterpiece", and it was the author's favourite of his own works.

Wells made a return to the genre of scientific romance with *In the Days of the Comet* (1906), which was also notable for its critique of the institution of marriage and apparent advocacy of free love, subjects already touched on in *A Modern Utopia*, among others. Willie Leadford quits his job as a clerk in a pottery firm, and then plots to murder the woman who has jilted him and her lover. However, just as he is about to execute his plan, a comet enters the Earth's atmosphere, discharging a mysterious green fog that sends Leadford, along with everyone else on the planet, to sleep. When he awakes he finds that, due to the effects of the gas, his malice has evaporated, and instead he feels only compassion and warmth towards his fellow man. The transformation is universal, and human society is reorganized accordingly. The novel ends with Leadford apparently enjoying an open relationship involving his wife, the woman who jilted him and the latter's husband. *In the Days of the Comet* was widely criticized for its apparent endorsement of promiscuity, and damaged Wells's standing with the Fabians.

In the Days of the Comet

Perhaps Wells's most ambitious work of fiction in the realist mode was *Tono-Bungay*, which was serialized in the *English Review*, a new journal founded by Ford Madox Ford, from December 1908, before being published in book form in 1909. It consisted of the picaresque adventures of another Wellsian "little man", George Ponderevo, and was reminiscent in its satirical scope of the "condition of England" novels of the previous century. After a humble start in life as a baker's apprentice, Ponderevo is employed by his uncle Edward to market a patent medicine called "Tono-Bungay", despite believing it to be a "damned swindle" – which it is. Commercial success and prosperity ensue, but Ponderevo leaves the enterprise to study aeronautics. When his uncle's business empire collapses, Ponderevo seeks to rescue him by embarking on an expedition to an island off the coast of West Africa to steal a radioactive compound called "quap", but the endeavour fails when the substance destroys the ship. Further adventures follow as Ponderevo attempts to save his uncle's fortunes. The novel was fundamentally pessimistic about the state of English society in the Edwardian period; as Ponderevo says towards the end, "I see decay all about me because I am, in a sense, decay."

Tono-Bungay

Published in the same year as *Tono-Bungay*, *Ann Veronica* was another *roman à clef*, although this time Wells drew on more recent experiences – rather than his early life – for inspiration, in a way that proved controversial. The titular character is a precocious and independent-minded twenty-one-year-old who, after quarrelling with her father, leaves her suburban home to move to central London, where she studies biology at Imperial College and becomes a passionate suffragette. When she falls

Ann Veronica

in love with an older and married man, Capes, the couple's relationship seems doomed, but Capes, who reciprocates Ann Veronica's feelings, relents and leaves his wife. At the end the couple are happily cohabiting, and Ann Veronica is pregnant and reconciled with her family. The story was transparently autobiographical, echoing both the author's elopement with Jane, the student who became his second wife, and his ongoing affair with the young Fabian Amber Reeves (clearly the model for Ann Veronica), for whom he was contemplating leaving Jane. Sensation accompanied the book's publication; in the words of Wells's son, Anthony West, this was because it could be read as "a self-serving justification of his own scandalous behaviour". Correctly anticipating controversy, Frederick Macmillan refused to publish the novel; it went instead to T. Fisher Unwin.

The History of Mr Polly

The History of Mr Polly (1910) was a return to the comic realism of *Kipps*, once again with autobiographical elements, and once again taking the form of a fantasy of escape from an unfulfilling life. Alfred Polly, the latest iteration of the downtrodden petit bourgeois so common in Wells's fiction, is a frustrated owner of a draper's shop in the fictional town of Fishbourne in Kent and married to his nagging cousin, Miriam Larkin. Faced with bankruptcy, Polly decides to burn down his shop and take his own life, but bungles it, inadvertently becoming a local hero when he rescues his mother-in-law from the fire. Thereafter he pursues a life on the road, eventually finding contentment as an innkeeper. *The History of Mr Polly* is widely considered a masterpiece.

The New Machiavelli

Wells's next novel was, like *The History of Mr Polly*, something of an escapist fantasy with autobiographical elements, although this time, as with *Ann Veronica*, the parallels between art and life proved somewhat controversial. *The New Machiavelli* tells the story of Dick Remington, a member of Parliament who abandons his wife and career to pursue his relationship with a brilliant young Oxford graduate, Isabel Rivers. That Isabel was based on Amber Reeves was perfectly obvious, and the satirical portraits of Sidney and Beatrice Webb in the characters of the Baileys, a socialist couple who influence Remington's politics, were obvious. Despite initially agreeing to publish on the understanding that it was a political novel, Macmillan again rejected Wells's manuscript when he became aware of the sexual content. Others, including Heinemann, were also unwilling to associate themselves with the gossip surrounding Wells's private life, although a publisher was eventually found in the form of the Bodley Head, a house famous for *The Yellow Book* in the 1890s and known for literary controversy. The book appeared in 1911 after being serialized in the *English Review* the previous year.

With *The World Set Free* (1914), Wells produced a work of prophecy in the vein of *In the Days of the Comet* about a cataclysmic event that brings about a restructuring of human society and culture. A future war between two power blocs, the Free Nations and the Central Powers, results in the invention of "atomic bombs" that devastate the world, although this apocalypse is followed by the formation of a single and ideal world state in place of the multitude of competing nations. As before in Wells's prophecies, the new order is led by an enlightened elite. The technological dimension was inspired by the English radiochemist Frederick Soddy's *Interpretation of Radium* (1909), to which the novel is dedicated; in turn, it may have influenced the development of nuclear weapons: the Hungarian physicist Leo Szilard, the inventor in 1933 of the nuclear chain reaction, claimed to have read and been inspired by the book.

The World Set Free

The satirical *Boon* (1915), which purports to be the work of its fictional narrator, Reginald Bliss (Wells was only credited as the author of the introduction), is notable for being the culmination of Wells's disagreement with his friend Henry James about the nature of literature. It is given the form of a memorial volume consisting of the literary remains of a recently deceased popular author named George Boon, which supposedly have been edited for publication by Bliss, his literary executor. Among other parodies and sketches, one of the chapters is a vindictive and explicit critique of the Jamesian style: "His vast paragraphs sweat and struggle... And all for tales of nothingness." James was deeply hurt and, despite Wells's attempts to apologize and to pass the piece off as a *jeu d'esprit*, never forgave his former friend for his "bad manners". James died the next year.

Boon

By 1916 Wells had come to repent of the jingoistic support for the campaign against Germany that he had expressed at the time of the outbreak of the First World War two years earlier, and provided an account of his change of heart in a transparent *roman à clef*. Britling, a famous author, writes an intemperate article supporting the war in 1914, but – not least because of the death of his son Hugh in the trenches (a departure from autobiographical fidelity) – becomes despondent, eventually placing his hope instead in the project for a "League of Free Nations". Britling also finds faith in a version of a Christian God he calls "the Captain of Mankind", a conversion apparently signifying the author's own, although the agnostic Wells later described this as an aberration. *Mr Britling Sees It Through* was a huge commercial hit: there were thirteen print runs in the year of publication, and Wells was paid US royalties of £20,000. It was also a critical success, winning praise from, among others, John Galsworthy and Maxim Gorky.

Mr Britling Sees It Through

The Outline of History

Towards the end of the First World War, disillusioned by his experience of working for the government's propaganda operation, Wells sought to reinvent himself as an educator, intent on mankind's "salvation by history". He conceived an ambitious chronicle of human civilization, an "account of man's story in the universe", and set about, with the help of his wife Jane, synthesizing the contents of existing reference works, notably the *Encyclopaedia Britannica*, enlisting the help of experts – including scholars like Ernest Barker and Gilbert Murray – to review his drafts and correct his errors. The work was designed to reflect Wells's own world view – namely, as he wrote in an article, that the peoples of the world "are all engaged in a common work... have sprung from common origins and are all contributing some special service to the general end" – a reiteration of Wells's belief in the need for global unity. *The Outline of History* first appeared in twenty-four illustrated fortnightly instalments from November 1919 before being published as a single volume in 1920. It was the first of several educational textbooks, including *A Short History of the World* (1922), *The Science of Life* (1930) and *The Work, Wealth and Happiness of Mankind* (1931).

The World of William Clissold

The World of William Clissold (1926) was Wells's longest novel, published in three volumes. It was another *roman à clef*, this time reflecting the author's relationship with Odette Keun. William Clissold, a wealthy industrialist, has retired to the south of France, where he recounts the story of his life, including his unhappy marriage, affairs and current relationship with Clementina (based on Odette), a young woman of Scottish and Greek ancestry. The last section of the novel is a description of Clissold's (and therefore Wells's) idea for a global "open conspiracy" of industrialists and other powerful figures, dedicated to the establishment of a "world republic" – "to be effected without the support of the crowd and possibly in spite of its dissent". Wells developed this idea further in a non-fiction work, *The Open Conspiracy* (1928).

The Shape of Things to Come

Partly in response to the deteriorating world situation, in 1933 Wells wrote *The Shape of Things to Come*, a science-fiction work purporting to be written by a diplomat from the League of Nations, Dr Philip Raven, who has had dreams in which he has been able to read a historical textbook written a century and a half in the future and describing world events from the First World War to the early twenty-second century. In it Wells imagined the outbreak of a second world war in 1939, stemming from a dispute between Germany and Poland over Danzig, which lays waste to civilization before ending inconclusively in 1950, to be followed first by a devastating plague and then by a technocratic "dictatorship of the air", a benign tyranny led by airmen that imposes order before being replaced by a characteristically Wellsian utopia. *Things to Come*, an ambitious cinematic adaptation of *The Shape of Things to Come*, appeared two years later, in 1936, a collaboration between Wells and the Hungarian filmmaker Alexander Korda.

Wells's last book, *Mind at the End of Its Tether* (1944), written when the author was seventy-eight and apparently bereft of hope for the future, was short and apocalyptic, describing the revolt against life on earth by nature, or what Wells calls "the Antagonist" and the "unknown implacable": "the end of everything we call life is close at hand and cannot be evaded."

Mind at the End of Its Tether

Select Bibliography

Autobiographies and Correspondence:
Experiment in Autobiography, 2 vols. (London: Gollancz, 1934)
H.G. Wells in Love: Postscript to An Experiment in Autobiography, ed. G.P. Wells (London: Faber, 1984)
The Correspondence of H.G. Wells, ed. David C. Smith, 4 vols (London: Pickering & Chatto, 1998)

Biographies:
Foot, Michael, *H.G.: The History of Mr Wells* (London: Doubleday, 1995)
MacKenzie, Norman and Jeanne, *The Time Traveller: The Life of H.G. Wells* (London: Weidenfeld & Nicolson, 1973)
Sherborne, Michael, *H.G. Wells: Another Kind of Life* (London: Peter Owen, 2010)
Smith, David C., *H.G. Wells: Desperately Mortal* (New Haven: Yale University Press, 1987)
Wells, Frank, *H.G. Wells: A Pictorial Biography* (London: Jupiter, 1977)
West, Anthony, *H.G. Wells: Aspects of a Life* (New York: Random House, 1984)

Additional Recommended Background Material:
Hammond, John, *An H.G. Wells Companion* (London: Macmillan, 1979)
Lodge, David, *A Man of Parts* (London: Harvill Secker, 2011)
Parrinder, Patrick, *H.G. Wells: The Critical Heritage* (London: Routledge & Kegan Paul, 1972)

EVERGREENS SERIES
Greatly produced classics, affordably priced

Jane Austen	*Emma*
	Mansfield Park
	Persuasion
	Sense and Sensibility
	Pride and Prejudice
Giovanni Boccaccio	*Decameron*
Charlotte Brontë	*Jane Eyre*
Emily Brontë	*Wuthering Heights*
Miguel de Cervantes	*Don Quixote*
Wilkie Collins	*The Moonstone*
	The Woman in White
Joseph Conrad	*Heart of Darkness*
Dante Alighieri	*Inferno*
	Purgatory
Charles Dickens	*A Christmas Carol and Other Christmas Stories*
	Great Expectations
	Hard Times
	Oliver Twist
Fyodor Dostoevsky	*The Double*
	The Gambler
	The Idiot
	Notes from Underground
Erasmus	*Praise of Folly*
F. Scott Fitzgerald	*The Great Gatsby*

Gustave Flaubert	*Madame Bovary*
Ford Madox Ford	*The Good Soldier*
J.W. von Goethe	*The Sorrows of Young Werther*
Nikolai Gogol	*Petersburg Tales*
Thomas Hardy	*Tess of the d'Urbervilles*
Nathaniel Hawthorne	*The Scarlet Letter*
Henry James	*The Portrait of a Lady*
Franz Kafka	*The Metamorphosis and Other Stories*
D.H. Lawrence	*Lady Chatterley's Lover*
Mikhail Lermontov	*A Hero of Our Time*
Niccolò Machiavelli	*The Prince*
Edgar Allan Poe	*Tales of Horror*
Alexander Pushkin	*Eugene Onegin*
William Shakespeare	*Sonnets*
Mary Shelley	*Frankenstein*
Robert L. Stevenson	*Strange Case of Dr Jekyll and Mr Hyde and Other Stories*
Jonathan Swift	*Gulliver's Travels*
Antal Szerb	*Journey by Moonlight*
Leo Tolstoy	*Anna Karenina*
Ivan Turgenev	*Fathers and Children*
Mark Twain	*Adventures of Huckleberry Finn* *The Adventures of Tom Sawyer*
Oscar Wilde	*The Picture of Dorian Gray*
Virginia Woolf	*Mrs Dalloway*
Stefan Zweig	*A Game of Chess and Other Stories*

**Order online for a 20% discount at
www.almaclassics.com**

ALMA CLASSICS

ALMA CLASSICS aims to publish mainstream and lesser-known European classics in an innovative and striking way, while employing the highest editorial and production standards. By way of a unique approach the range offers much more, both visually and textually, than readers have come to expect from contemporary classics publishing.

LATEST TITLES PUBLISHED BY ALMA CLASSICS

398 William Makepeace Thackeray, *Vanity Fair*
399 Jules Verne, *A Fantasy of Dr Ox*
400 Anonymous, *Beowulf*
401 Oscar Wilde, *Selected Plays*
402 Alexander Trocchi, *The Holy Man and Other Stories*
403 Charles Dickens, *David Copperfield*
404 Cyrano de Bergerac, *A Voyage to the Moon*
405 Jack London, *White Fang*
406 Antonin Artaud, *Heliogabalus, or The Anarchist Crowned*
407 John Milton, *Paradise Lost*
408 James Fenimore Cooper, *The Last of the Mohicans*
409 Charles Dickens, *Mugby Junction*
410 Robert Louis Stevenson, *Kidnapped*
411 Paul Éluard, *Selected Poems*
412 Alan Burns, *Dreamerika!*
413 Thomas Hardy, *Jude the Obscure*
414 Virginia Woolf, *Flush*
415 Abbé Prevost, *Manon Lescaut*
416 William Blake, *Selected Poems*
417 Alan Riddell, *Eclipse: Concrete Poems*
418 William Wordsworth, *The Prelude and Other Poems*
419 Tobias Smollett, *The Expedition of Humphry Clinker*
420 Pablo Picasso, *The Three Little Girls and Desire Caught by the Tail*
421 Nikolai Gogol, *The Government Inspector*
422 Rudyard Kipling, *Kim*
423 Jean-Paul Sartre, *Politics and Literature*
424 Matthew Lewis, *The Monk*
425 Ambrose Bierce, *The Devil's Dictionary*
426 Frances Hodgson Burnett, *A Little Princess*
427 Walt Whitman, *Leaves of Grass*
428 Daniel Defoe, *Moll Flanders*
429 Mary Wollstonecraft, *The Vindications*
430 Anonymous, *The Song of Roland*
431 Edward Lear, *The Owl and the Pussycat and Other Nonsense Poetry*
432 Anton Chekhov, *Three Years*
433 Fyodor Dostoevsky, *Uncle's Dream*

www.almaclassics.com